Mary Higgins Clark

and

Carol Higgins Clark

Deck the Halls

BOOKSPAN LARGE PRINT EDITION

Simon & Schuster / Scribner
New York London Toronto Sydney Singapore

This Large Print Edition, prepared especially for
Bookspan, contains the complete, unabridged
text of the original Publisher's Edition.

 SIMON & SCHUSTER / SCRIBNER
Rockefeller Center
1230 Avenue of the Americas
New York, NY 10020

Copyright © 2000 by Mary Higgins Clark and
Carol Higgins Clark
All rights reserved, including the right of reproduction in
whole or in part in any form.

SIMON & SCHUSTER and colophon are registered
trademarks of Simon & Schuster, Inc.

Manufactured in the United States of America

ISBN 0-7394-1383-X

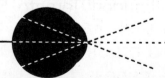

This Large Print Book carries the
Seal of Approval of N.A.V.H.

Acknowledgments

Now that the tale is told, we are frequently asked, "Was it hard to work together?"

The answer is "No." It was fun. By the time we got to the closing pages, we were so in tandem that if we were searching for a descriptive word, we often would come out with the same one in the same breath.

Of course the journey was made smoother by the help and encouragement of others.

And so we joyfully deck the halls for our editors, Michael Korda, Chuck Adams, and Roz Lippel.

A glittering ornament for Lisl Cade, our publicist.

Silvery garlands for Associate Director of Copyediting Gypsy da Silva, copy editor Carol Catt, proofreaders Barbara Raynor and Steve Friedeman, and at Dix!, Account Executive Kelly Farley, keyboarder Dwayne Harris, and proofreader Barbara Decker.

Candy canes for our agents Gene Winick, Sam Pinkus, and Nick Ellison.

A cup of cheer for our law enforcement experts, Sgt. Steve Marron and Detective

Richard Murphy, Ret., New York District Attorney's Office.

A holiday kiss for Santa's helpers, better known as our family and friends, especially John Conheeney, Irene Clark, Agnes Newton, and Nadine Petry.

And a holiday greeting to our readers. May your days be merry and bright.

God bless . . .

In the spirit of this shared journey,
we, Mary and Carol,
are dedicating this book to each other
with love.

Deck the Halls

Thursday, December 22nd

Regan Reilly sighed for the hundredth time as she looked down at her mother, Nora, a brand-new patient in Manhattan's Hospital for Special Surgery. "And to think I bought you that dopey crocheted rug you tripped on," she said.

"You only bought it. I caught my heel in it," the well-known mystery writer said wanly. "It wasn't your fault I was wearing those idiotic stilts."

Nora attempted to shift her body, which was anchored by a heavy plaster cast that reached from her toes to her thigh.

"I'll leave you two to assess the blame for the broken leg," Luke Reilly, owner of three funeral homes, husband and father, observed as he hoisted his long, lean body from the low bedside armchair. "I've got a funeral to go to, a dentist's appointment, and then, since our Christmas plans are somewhat altered, I guess I'd better see about buying a tree."

He bent over and kissed his wife. "Look at it this way: you may not be gazing at the Pacific Ocean, but you've got a good view of the East River." He and Nora and their only child, thirty-one-year-old Regan, had been planning to spend the Christmas holiday on Maui.

"You're a scream," Nora told him. "Dare we hope you'll arrive home with a tree that isn't your usual Charlie Brown special?"

"That's not nice," Luke protested.

"But it's true." Nora dismissed the subject. "Luke, you look exhausted. Can't you skip Goodloe's funeral? Austin can take care of everything."

Austin Grady was Luke's right-hand man. He had handled hundreds of funerals on his own, but the one today was different. The deceased, Cuthbert Boniface Goodloe, had left the bulk of his estate to the Seed-Plant-Bloom-and-Blossom Society of the Garden State of New Jersey. His disgruntled nephew and partial namesake, Cuthbert Boniface Dingle, known as C.B., was obviously bitter about his meager inheritance. After viewing hours yesterday afternoon, C.B. had sneaked back to the casket where Luke had found him stuffing rotted bits of house plants in the sleeves of the pin-striped designer suit the fastidious Goodloe had chosen as his last outfit.

As Luke came up behind C.B., he heard him whispering, "You love plants? I'll give you plants, you senile old hypocrite. Get a whiff of these! Enjoy them from now until Resurrection Day!"

Luke had backed away, not wanting to confront C.B., who continued to vent verbal outrage at the body of his less-than-generous uncle. It was not the first time Luke had heard a mourner telling off the deceased, but the use of decaying foliage was a first. Later, Luke had quietly removed the offensive vegetation. But today, he wanted to keep an eye on C.B. himself. Besides, he hadn't had a chance to mention the incident to Austin.

Luke considered telling Nora about the nephew's bizarre behavior, but then decided not to go into it. "Goodloe's been planning his own funeral with me for three years," he said instead. "If I didn't show up, he'd haunt me."

"I suppose you should go." Nora's voice was sleepy, and her eyes were starting to close. "Regan, why don't you let Dad drop you off at the apartment? The last painkiller they gave me is knocking me out."

"I'd rather hang around until your private nurse gets here," Regan said. "I want to make sure someone is with you."

"All right. But then go to the apartment and crash. You know you never sleep on the red-eye flight."

Regan, a private investigator who lived in Los Angeles, had been packing for the trip to Hawaii when her father phoned.

"Your mother's fine," he began. "But she's had an accident. She broke her leg."

"She broke her leg?" Regan had repeated.

"Yes. We were on our way to a black tie at the Plaza. Mom was one of the honorees. She was running a little late. I rang for the elevator . . ."

One of Dad's not very subtle ways of getting Mom to hurry up, Regan thought.

"The elevator arrived, but she didn't. I

went back into the apartment and found her lying on the floor with her leg at a very peculiar angle. But you know your mother. Her first question was to ask if her gown was torn."

That would be Mom, Regan had thought affectionately.

"She was the best-dressed emergency-room patient in the history of the hospital," Luke had concluded.

Regan had dumped her Hawaii clothes out of the suitcase and replaced them with winter clothes suitable for New York. She barely made the last night flight from Los Angeles to Kennedy, and once in New York had paused only long enough to drop off her bags at her parents' apartment on Central Park South.

From the doorway of the hospital room, Luke looked back and smiled at the sight of the two women in his life, so alike in some ways with their classic features, blue eyes, and fair skin, but so different in others. From the Black Irish Reillys, Regan had inherited raven black hair, a throw-back to the Spaniards who had settled in Ireland after their Armada had been destroyed in battle with the British. Nora, however, was a natural blonde, and at five feet three inches was four inches shorter than her daughter. At six feet five, Luke towered over both of them. His once-dark hair was now almost completely silver.

"Regan, I'll meet you back here at around seven," he said. "After we cheer your mother up, we'll go out and have a good dinner."

He caught Nora's expression and smiled at her. "You thrive on the urge to kill, honey. All the reviewers say so." He waved his hand. "See you girls tonight."

It was a commitment Luke would not be able to keep.

Across town, apartment 16B at 211 Central Park South was in the process of being decorated for Christmas. "Deck the halls with boughs of holly," Alvirah Meehan sang, off-key, as she placed a miniature wreath around the framed picture of Willy and herself accepting the $40 million lottery check that had changed their lives forever.

The picture brought back vividly that magical evening three years ago, when she'd been sitting in their tiny living room in Flushing, Queens, and Willy had been half asleep in his old club chair. She had been soaking her feet in a pail of warm water after a hard day of cleaning Mrs. O'Keefe's house when Willy came home, really bushed, from repairing a burst pipe that had sent showers of rusty water on the newly pressed clothes at Spot-Free Dry Cleaners down the block. Then the announcer on television began to read the winning lottery numbers.

I sure look different now, Alvirah thought, shaking her head as she examined the picture. The brassy red hair that for so many years she had dyed herself in the bathroom sink had been transformed by Madame Judith, to a soft golden red with subtle shadings. The purple polyester pants suit had long ago been banished by her classy friend, Baroness Min Von Schreiber. Of course, her jutting jaw was the same, a product of God's design when he molded her, but she'd gotten down from a size sixteen to a trimmer size fourteen. There was no question about it—she looked ten years younger and a thousand times better now than in the old days.

I was sixty then and looked like I was pushing seventy. Now I'm sixty-three and don't look a day over fifty-nine, she told herself happily. On the other hand, she decided, looking at the picture, even dressed in that bargain-basement blue suit and skinny little tie, Willy managed to look handsome and distinguished. With his shock of white hair and vivid blue eyes, Willy always reminded people of the late, legendary Speaker of the House of Representatives, Tip O'Neill.

Poor Willy, she sighed. What bad luck that he feels so rotten. Nobody should be stuck with a toothache during the Christmas season. But Dr. Jay will fix him up. Our big mistake was to get involved with that other guy when Dr. Jay moved to New Jersey, Alvirah thought. He talked Willy into getting a dental implant even though it hadn't worked last time, and it's been killing him. Oh, well, it could be worse, she reminded herself. Look what happened to Nora Regan Reilly.

She had heard on the radio that the suspense author, who happened to be her favorite writer, had broken her leg the evening before in her apartment in the very next building. Her high heel had caught in the fringe of a rug, Alvirah mused—the same kind of thing that happened to Grandma. But Grandma wasn't wearing high heels. She had stepped on a wad of bubble gum in the street, and when the fringe of the rug stuck to the bottom of her orthopedic sneakers, she went sprawling.

"Hi, honey." Willy was coming down the hall from the bedroom. The right side of his face was swollen, and his expression was instant testimony to the fact that the troublesome implant was still killing him.

Alvirah knew how to cheer him up. "Willy, you know what makes me feel good?"

"Whatever it is, share it right away."

"It's knowing that Dr. Jay will get rid of that implant, and by tonight you'll be feeling much better. I mean, aren't you better off than poor Nora Regan Reilly, who'll be hobbling around on crutches for weeks?"

Willy shook his head and managed a smile. "Alvirah, can I never have an ache or a pain without you telling me how lucky I am? If I came down with the bubonic plague, you'd try to make me feel sorry for somebody else."

Alvirah laughed. "I suppose I would at that," she agreed.

"When you ordered the car, did you allow for holiday traffic? I never thought I'd be worried about missing a dentist appointment, but today I am."

"Of course I did," she assured him. "We'll be there long before three. Dr. Jay squeezed you in before he sees his last patient. He's closing early for the holiday weekend."

Willy looked at his watch. "It's only a little after ten. I wish he could see me this minute. What time is the car coming?"

"One-thirty."

"I'll start to get ready."

With a sympathetic shake of her head, Alvirah watched her husband of forty-three years disappear back into the bedroom. He'll be feeling a thousand percent better tonight, she decided. I'll make some nice vegetable soup for dinner, and we'll watch the tape of *It's a Wonderful Life.* I'm glad we delayed our cruise until February. It will be good to have a quiet, at-home Christmas this year.

Alvirah looked around the room and sniffed appreciatively. I love the smell of pine, she thought. And the tree looks gorgeous. They had placed it right in the center of the floor-to-ceiling windows overlooking Central Park. The branches were laden with the ornaments they'd accumulated over the years, some handsome, some battered, all cherished. Alvirah pushed back her large, round glasses, walked over to the cocktail table, and grabbed the last unopened box of tinsel.

"You never can have too much tinsel on the tree," she said aloud.

Three more days until Christmas, twenty-six-year-old Rosita Gonzalez thought, as she waited for Luke Reilly behind the wheel of one of the Reilly Funeral Home limos, standing near the hospital's Seventy-first Street entrance. Mentally she reviewed the presents she had bought for her five- and six-year-old sons, Bobby and Chris. I haven't forgotten anything, she assured herself.

She so wanted them to have a good Christmas. So much had changed in the last year and a half. Their father had left—not that that was any loss—and her ailing mother had moved back to Puerto Rico. Now both boys clung to Rosita as if they were afraid *she* would somehow disappear too.

My little guys, she thought with a rush of tenderness. Together, the three of them had picked out their Christmas tree last night and would decorate it tonight. She had the next three days off, and Mr. Reilly had given her a generous Christmas bonus.

Rosita looked in the rearview mirror and straightened the driver's cap over her waterfall of dark curly hair. It sure was a stroke of luck when I got the job at the funeral home, she thought. She had started working part-time in the office, but when Luke learned that she moonlighted as a limo driver, he told her, "You can have all the extra work you want here, Rosita." Now she frequently drove for funerals.

There was a tap on the driver's window. Rosita looked up, expecting to see the face of her good-natured boss. Instead she found herself locking eyes with a vaguely familiar countenance, which, for the moment, she could not place. She opened the window a few inches and was rewarded with a belch of cigarette smoke. His head darting forward, her unexpected visitor identified himself in staccato tones: "Hi, Rosie, I'm Petey the Painter. Remember me?"

How could I forget? Rosita wondered. A mental image of the brilliant chartreuse shade he'd painted the main viewing room of the Reilly funeral home in Summit, New Jersey, flashed through her mind. She remembered Luke Reilly's reaction when he saw it. "Rosita," Luke had said, "I don't know whether to laugh, cry, or throw up."

"I'd throw up, Mr. Reilly," had been Rosita's advice.

Needless to say, Petey the Painter's services had no longer been requested nor required in any of the three Reilly funeral homes.

Petey had gratuitously added bright yellow to the moss-green paint Luke had selected, declaring that he thought the place needed a little livening. "Relatives of dead people need cheering up," he'd informed them. "That green was really depressing. I had a little extra yellow paint in my car, so

I threw it in for free." On his way out, he'd asked Rosita for a date, which she'd promptly declined.

Rosita wondered if he still had flecks of paint in his hair. She looked at him, but couldn't tell. A cap with earmuffs covered every inch of his head and shaded his narrow, bony face. His wiry frame was encased in a dark-blue storm jacket. The turned-up collar of the jacket grazed the graying stubble that shaded his chin.

"Of course I remember you, Petey," she said. "What are you doing here?"

He shuffled from foot to foot. "You look great, Rosie. Too bad your most important passengers never get to feast their eyes on you."

The reference, of course, was to the fact that Rosita sometimes drove the hearse in funeral cortèges.

"You're funny, Petey. See you." She began to raise the window but was stopped by Petey's hand.

"Hey, it's freezing out. Can I sit in the car? I need to ask you something."

"Petey, Mr. Reilly will be here any minute."

"This will only take a minute," he explained.

Reluctantly, Rosita threw the lock that opened all the doors. She had expected him to go around and get in beside her in the front seat. Instead, in a lightning-fast motion, he opened the back door of the vehicle and slid in.

Thoroughly annoyed with her intruder, she swiveled her head around to face him in the back of the limo, whose tinted windows shielded anyone seated there from the view of the outside world. What she saw took her breath away. For a moment she thought it was a joke. Surely that couldn't be a gun Petey was holding?

"Nobody's going to get hurt if you do what I tell you," Petey said soothingly. "Just keep a nice, calm look on your pretty face until the King of the Stiffs gets here."

A weary and preoccupied Luke Reilly emerged from the elevator and walked the short distance to the door of the hospital, barely noticing the Christmas decorations adorning the lobby. He stepped outside into the raw, cloudy morning and was glad to see his limo waiting near the end of the driveway.

In a few strides, Luke's long legs brought him to the car. He knocked on the window of the passenger side, and a moment later was turning the handle of the back door. He was inside and had closed the door behind him before he realized that he was not alone in the backseat.

Luke's unerring memory for faces, coupled with the sight of paint-flecked boots, made him realize instantly that the man sitting opposite him with the gun in his hand was none other than the idiot who had turned his viewing room into a psychedelic nightmare.

"In case you don't remember me, I'm Petey the Painter. I worked for you last summer." Petey raised his voice. "Start driving, Rosie," he ordered. "Turn right at the corner and pull over. We're making a pickup."

"I remember you," Luke said quietly. "But I prefer seeing you with a paintbrush instead of a gun. What's this all about?"

"My friend will explain when he gets in. Nice comfortable car you got here."

Again, Petey raised his voice. "Rosie, don't try any funny stuff like running a light. We don't want no attention from the cops."

Luke had barely slept the night before, and his mind was blurry. Now he felt somehow detached from reality, as though he were dreaming or half asleep, watching a movie. He was alert enough, however, to sense that this unlikely kidnapper might never have held a gun before, which actually made him twice as dangerous. Luke knew he could not take the chance of throwing himself forward in an attempt to overpower his captor.

Rosie turned the corner. The car had not quite stopped when the front passenger door opened and another man joined them. Luke's mouth dropped: Petey the Painter's partner in crime was none other than C. B. Dingle, the disgruntled nephew of the late Cuthbert Boniface Goodloe.

Like Petey, C.B. was wearing a cap with earmuffs that fit loosely over his balding head, and a bulky, nondescript storm jacket that covered his butterball-shaped torso. C.B.'s round, pale face was half covered by a dark, bushy mustache that had not been present at his uncle's wake the day before. Wincing, he pulled off the fuzzy disguise and addressed Luke.

"Thank you for being on time," he said cordially as he patted his lip. "I don't want to be late for my uncle's funeral. But I'm afraid *you're* not going to make it, Mr. Reilly."

Where are they taking us? Rosita agonized as, following C.B.'s instructions, she turned right on Ninety-sixth Street and headed for the FDR Drive north. She had seen C.B. at the funeral parlor only yesterday, had met him a couple of times before when he came to the funeral home with his uncle, who kept changing his mind about the plans for his last farewell.

Irrationally, she almost smiled, remembering that Cuthbert Boniface Goodloe had stopped in only last month to inform Luke that the restaurant he had chosen for a reception after his funeral had been closed down by the Health Department. She had driven Mr. Reilly, Goodloe, and C.B. to the Orchard Hill Inn, which Mr. Reilly had suggested as a replacement.

Mr. Reilly told her later that Goodloe had painstakingly studied the menu, eliminating the most expensive items from his guests' future selections.

That day C.B., as usual, had been practically kissing his uncle's butt, which obviously had done him no good. Yesterday afternoon the viewing room had been filled with shocked but grateful members of the Seed-Plant-Bloom-and-Blossom Society of the Garden State of New Jersey—a group commonly known as the Blossoms—whose goal to spruce up every nook and cranny of New Jersey had just received a much needed million-dollar shot in the arm. The buzz was that Goodloe's dying words to his nephew had been, "Get a job!"

Had C.B. gone crazy? Was he dangerous? And what does he want with me and Mr. Reilly? Rosita wondered as, even inside her gloves, her fingers turned to ice.

"Head for the George Washington Bridge," C.B. ordered.

At least they were going back to New Jersey, Rosita thought. She wondered if there was any hope of appealing to C.B. to let them go.

"Mr. Dingle, you may know I have two little boys who need me," she said softly. "They're five and six years old, and their father hasn't supported or seen them in over a year."

"My father was a crumb too," C.B. snapped. "And don't call me Mr. Dingle. I hate that name."

Petey had overheard. "It's a dumb name," he agreed. "But your first and middle names are even worse. Thank God for initials. Mr. Reilly, can you believe C.B.'s mom saddled him with a name like Cuthbert Boniface, in honor of her sister's husband. And then, when the old geezer passes away, he gives just about everything to the stupid Blossoms? Maybe they'll name a new strain of poison ivy after him."

"I spent my whole life pretending to like those stupid names!" C.B. said angrily. "And what do I get for it? Career advice three seconds before he croaks."

"I'm sorry about all that, C.B.," Luke said firmly. "But your problems have nothing to do with us. Why are we here, or more precisely, why are you and Petey in my car?"

"I beg to differ—" C.B. began.

Petey interrupted: "I really like that expression. It sounds so classy."

"Shut up, Petey," C.B. snapped. "My problem has *everything* to do with you, Mr. Reilly. But your wife is going to have a million ways to make it up."

They were halfway across the George Washington Bridge.

"Petey, you tell Rosie where to turn. You know the way better than I do."

"Take the Fort Lee exit," Petey began. "We're going south."

Fifteen minutes later, the car pulled onto a narrow road that led down to the Hudson River. Rosita was on the verge of tears. They reached an empty parking area at the river's edge, facing the skyline of Manhattan. To the left they could see the towering gray span of the George Washington Bridge. The heavy stream of holiday traffic crossing back and forth on its two levels only increased Rosita's sense of isolation. She had a sudden terrible fear that C.B. and Petey might be planning to shoot them and throw their bodies into the river.

"Get out of the car," C.B. ordered. "Remember we both have guns and know how to use them."

Petey aimed his revolver at Luke's head as he and Rosita reluctantly left the familiarity of the car. He gave the weapon a quick twirl. "I watched reruns of *The Rifleman* doing this," he explained. "I'm getting real good at twirling."

Luke shuddered.

"I'll be your escort," C.B. told him. "We have to hurry. I have a funeral to make."

They were forced to walk along the shore, past a deserted marina, to where a dilapidated houseboat, its windows boarded up, was anchored at the end of a narrow dock. The boat rocked up and down, as the river lapped restlessly against its sides. It was obvious to Luke that the worn and aging craft was sitting dangerously low in the water.

"Take a look at the ice that's starting to form out there. You can't be planning to put us on that thing in this weather," Luke protested.

"In summertime it's real nice," Petey boasted. "I take care of it for the guy who owns it. He's in Arizona for the winter. His arthritis is something awful."

"This isn't July," Luke snapped.

"Sometimes you get bad weather in July too," Petey responded. "One time there was a real bad storm, and—"

"Shut up, Petey," C.B. growled irritably. "I told you, you talk too much."

"You would too if you painted rooms all by yourself twelve hours a day. When I'm with people, I like to talk."

C.B. shook his head. "He drives me nuts," he said under his breath. "Now be careful getting onto the boat," he told Rosita. "I don't want you to slip."

"You can't do this to us. I've got to go home to my boys," Rosita cried.

Luke could hear the note of hysteria in Rosita's voice. The poor kid is scared stiff, he thought. Just a few years younger than Regan and supporting two children on her own. "Help her!" he barked.

Petey used his free hand to grasp Rosita's arm as, fearfully, she stepped down onto the deck of the swaying vessel.

"You're very good at influencing people, Mr. Reilly," C.B. complimented. "Let's hope you're as successful for the next twenty-four hours."

Petey unlocked the door of the cabin

and pushed it open, releasing a dank, musty smell into the cold outside air.

"Whew," Petey said. "That stink'll get you every time."

"Move it, Petey," C.B. ordered. "I told you to get an Airwick."

"How thoughtful," Rosita said sarcastically as she followed Petey inside.

Luke glanced over at the Manhattan skyline, then looked upriver to the George Washington Bridge, taking in the little red lighthouse underneath. I wonder if I'll ever get the chance to see all this again, he thought, as C.B. pressed the gun in the small of his back.

"Inside, Mr. Reilly. This isn't the time for sightseeing."

Petey turned on the dim overhead light as C.B. closed the door behind them.

On one side of the small, shabby space was a seating area consisting of a Formica dinette table surrounded by a cracked, imitation-leather banquette; directly opposite was a matching couch. The furniture was all built-in units. A small refrigerator, sink, and stove were adjacent to the table. Luke knew that the two doors to the left probably led to a bedroom and whatever passed for a bathroom.

"Oh, no," Rosita gasped.

Luke followed her stare, and with dismay realized that two sets of chains were bolted to the walls in the seating area. They were the kind of hand and ankle restraints commonly used to restrain criminal defendants in courtrooms. One set was next to the couch, the other near the banquette.

"You sit here," Petey directed Rosita. "Keep me covered, C.B., while I put her bracelets on."

"I got everybody covered," C.B. said emphatically. "You're over here, Mr. Reilly."

If I were alone, I'd take my chances and try to grab his gun, Luke thought angrily, but I can't risk Rosita's life. An instant later, he was sitting on the banquette, chained, with Rosita opposite him on the couch.

"I should have asked if either one of you cares to use the facilities, but now you'll just have to wait," C.B. said cheerfully. "I don't want to be late for my uncle's funeral. After all, I *am* the chief mourner. And

Petey needs to get rid of your car. When we come back, Petey'll bring stuff for your lunch. I won't be hungry, though. My uncle paid for my meal today, remember, Mr. Reilly?"

C.B. opened the door as Petey turned out the light. An instant later the door slammed shut, and Luke and Rosita could hear the grating of the key turning in the rusty lock.

Trapped in the shadowy darkness of the swaying boat, they both remained silent for a moment as the reality of their precarious situation hit both of them.

Then Rosita asked quietly, "Mr. Reilly, what's going to happen to us?"

Luke chose his words carefully. "They've already told us they're looking for money. Assuming that's all they really want, I promise it will be paid."

"All I can think about is my kids. My regular baby-sitter is away until next week, and I don't trust the girl who's filling in. Her Christmas dance is tonight. She didn't want to work at all today, but I begged her to. She expects me home by three."

"She wouldn't leave the boys alone."

"You don't know her, Mr. Reilly—she

won't miss that dance," Rosita said with certainty, a catch in her voice. "I've got to get home. I've just got to get home."

Regan opened her eyes, groggily sat up, swung her legs over the edge of the bed, and yawned. Her bedroom in her parents' apartment on Central Park South was as comfortably familiar as the one in the family home in New Jersey in which she'd been raised. Today, though, she did not take time to appreciate the charming ambience of the peach-and-soft-green color scheme. She had the sensation of having slept a long time, but when she looked at the clock, she was glad to see it was only a few minutes before two. She wanted to phone the hospital and see how her mother was doing, then catch up with her father. She realized that beyond the fact that she was feeling the effects of the news about her mother's accident and the hurried red-eye flight, she was filled with undefined anxiety. A quick shower might help me clear my mind, she thought, and then I'll get moving.

She put in a call to La Parisienne, the local coffee shop, and placed her usual breakfast order: orange juice, coffee, and a toasted bagel with cream cheese. This is what I love about New York, she thought. By the time I get out of the shower, the delivery boy will be ringing the bell.

The strong spray of hot water felt good on her back and shoulders. She quickly washed her hair, stepped out of the shower, wrapped herself in a robe, and rolled a towel around her head.

Ten seconds later, her face glistening with moisturizer, she answered the door for the delivery boy. She was glad he pretended not to notice her appearance. In his job, he's seen it all, she thought. But he did produce a sunny smile when she gave him a generous tip.

Moments later, the bagel unwrapped, the coffee cup in her hand, she phoned her mother's room. She knew the nurse had to be there, but no one picked up. The ringer is probably turned off, she thought. She hung up and dialed the nurses' station on that floor.

What seemed like several minutes passed as she waited for her mother's nurse to come to the phone. It was a relief to hear the friendly, professional, and re-assuring voice of Beverly Carter. She had come on duty this morning, just as Regan was leaving. Although they had spoken only briefly, Regan had instantly liked the slim, fortyish black woman, whom the doctor had introduced as one of their finest private nurses.

"Hi, Beverly. How's my mother?"

"She's been sleeping since you left."

"I've been sleeping since I left," Regan laughed. "When she wakes up, tell her I called. Have you heard from my father?"

"Not so far."

"I'm surprised. But he did have that fu-neral. I'll give him a call. Tell my mother she can always reach me on my cell phone."

Next, Regan dialed the funeral home. Austin Grady, the second in command at "Reilly's Remains," as Regan and her mother dubbed the funeral homes, an-swered. His initial greeting, as usual, was suitably subdued.

"Austin, it's Regan."

The somber tone turned jolly. "Regan, hello."

Regan was always amazed at the way

Austin could switch gears so rapidly, his demeanor of the moment dictated by the demands of his job. As Luke had observed, he was perfectly suited to this line of work. Like a surgeon, he was able to disassociate himself from surrounding emotions.

"Is my father there?" she asked.

"No, I haven't spoken to him since he called early this morning to send for a car. Your poor mother," he commiserated in a most upbeat tone. "What's going to happen next? And I know your father was really looking forward to the trip to Hawaii. I understand she tripped on a new rug you bought her in Ireland."

"Yes," Regan said quickly, guilt about her purchase washing over her again. As her best friend, Kit, always said, "Guilt is the gift that keeps on giving."

"Austin, my father told us he was going to be there for a funeral you were having today. Didn't he show up at all?"

"Well, no, but the service went beautifully. The old guy had been planning it for years. Your father probably realized he didn't really need to come." Austin chuckled. "Right now the mourners are all enjoying a free lunch across town. The deceased left the bulk of his estate to the Blossoms. They're all at the restaurant, and they look like one happy group. They inherited enough money to buy sprinkling cans for every plant in the state of New Jersey."

"Lucky them," Regan said.

"Your father has a 3:30 dentist's appointment on his schedule. I don't think he'll miss that."

"Thanks, Austin." Regan hung up and dialed Luke's cell phone. After several rings his voice mail came on. As she listened to her father's voice telling the caller to leave a message, her sense that something might be wrong deepened. Her father hadn't been heard from in hours, even to inquire about her mother. She left a message for him to call her.

She sipped her coffee and thought for a minute. I can't just sit here, she decided. She glanced at the clock. It was now 2:35. She called the dentist's office to confirm that her father had not canceled his appointment.

"Please ask him to wait for me," Regan said to the receptionist. "I'm leaving the city in a few minutes, and it shouldn't take me more than an hour to get there."

"Will do," the receptionist promised.

Regan hurriedly dressed and dried her hair. After Dad has his appointment, we can do the errands together, she thought. Then we'll drive back to the city to see Mom.

But even as she pulled on her coat and ran down to grab a cab, Regan somehow knew that that wasn't what she would be doing this afternoon.

How long had he and Rosita been locked up in the dark, chilly houseboat? Luke had no sense of time. It seemed like hours. They could have left the light on, he thought angrily.

After C.B. and Petey the Painter took off, Luke had tried to reassure Rosita. "Trust my hunch," he told her. "When those jerks come back, they'll tell us what they want. And when they get it, they'll let us go."

"But we can identify them, Mr. Reilly. Do you really think they can be that stupid?"

"Rosita, probably nobody else could be

that stupid, but I believe it of that pair. It won't be long before we're missed. Don't forget, my daughter's a private investigator, and she'll have everyone looking for us."

"Just as long as someone takes care of my kids. I'm so afraid that ditzy baby-sitter will dump them with someone they don't know. My little guy, especially, is painfully shy."

"If there's one thing I'm sure of, it's that when Regan realizes we're missing, she'll check on your kids."

They hadn't spoken for a while. It was only about ten feet across the cabin to the built-in couch where Rosita was chained. Had she dozed off? Luke wondered. The lapping of the water against the sides of the boat made it impossible to hear any sound of movement from her.

"Rosita," he said softly.

Before she could answer, a thud on the deck startled both of them. The sound of the key grating in the lock dispelled Luke's hope that whoever was outside might be a potential rescuer.

The door opened. A somber trickle of

light and a blast of cold air preceded Petey and C.B. into the cabin.

"How are our campers doing?" C.B. asked jovially as Petey snapped on the overhead light. "I hope you're not vegetarians. We bought ham and cheese sandwiches." Both men were carrying grocery bags.

It was with mixed emotion that Luke noted how small the bags were. Either they were planning to have them out of here in a short time, or there would be frequent take-outs from the local fast-food outlets in Edgewater.

"Either one of you want to go to the can?" Petey asked solicitously.

Luke and Rosita both nodded.

"Ladies first," Petey said. He released Rosita's hand and ankle shackles. "You can close the door, but don't get any stupid ideas. Besides, it don't have a window."

Rosita looked at Luke. "Could you lend me a dollar for the attendant?"

When it was Luke's turn inside the tiny cubicle, he considered his options and realized he had none. Even if he could overpower Petey when he was refastening the chains, C.B. would be standing with his gun trained on Rosita. I have to play along with them, he thought.

While Luke, Rosita, and Petey ate their sandwiches, C.B. sipped coffee. "I'm full," he said, looking at Luke. "That restaurant you suggested wasn't bad. The veal parmigiana was the best I've had in ages. Although I'm surprised I could digest my meal, having to look at those nerds from the Blossom Society. It was only the thought of you two back here that got me through."

"You could have brought me back some veal parmigiana," Petey griped. "I think this rye bread is a little stale. And he didn't put enough mayo on mine." He peered over at Luke's sandwich. "Let's switch halves."

Luke grabbed the second half of his sandwich and took a big bite out of it. He laid it back down on the wax paper. "Be my guest." Luke was inordinately pleased to see the disappointed look on Petey's face.

Petey looked at Rosita. "No dessert for the boss. You can have his Twinkies."

"I'd rather choke," Rosita snapped.

"Now that we're one big happy family, let's get down to business." C.B. crushed his empty coffee cup and stuffed it into the deli bag.

"Be careful, the pickles are still in there," Petey protested.

C.B. groaned and dumped the contents of the bag on the scarred Formica table.

"Don't get mad," Petey said. "I wasn't at some fancy lunch. I feel like I've been on a bus all day. Once I dumped the car at Kennedy, I had to take a bus to the Port Authority. Then I hadda wait for another bus to Edgewater. Then I hadda wait for you at the bus stop. You were too cheap to let me take a cab. *You've* been riding in a nice warm car all day—"

"Shut up!"

But Petey wasn't finished. "I had my four dollars ready to pay when I crossed the George Washington Bridge. Then when I'm waiting in a long line to hand it over, I discover there's an E-Z Pass on the floor of the car. I stuck it back up on the windshield and switched lanes fast. Some jerk almost plowed into me. He starts honking his horn like a crazy person. Then I saved you more money when I went over the Triborough Bridge. You should have noticed that E-Z Pass when you rode up front. I'm surprised at you."

C.B.'s eyes bulged. "You used the E-Z Pass? You moron! I took it off so they wouldn't be able to track us. Now they can check and find out where it's been used."

"Really?" Petey looked awestruck. "I'll be darned. What will they think of next?" He turned to Luke and Rosita. "C.B. is so smart. He reads a lot of detective novels. I never had much chance to read. Mr. Reilly, I know he really likes your wife's novels. I think one of them is even autographed."

"When you release us, I'll get him another one. And when is that going to happen?"

Petey reached for a pickle. "Explain our plan, C.B. It's so good. In a few days we're going to be on a beach somewhere with a million dollars in our suitcase."

C.B. interrupted Petey. "I'm telling you for the last time, Petey. Keep your mouth shut!" He pulled Luke's and Rosita's cell phones from the leather pouch where he had stashed them. "Mr. Reilly, it's nearly 4:30. We're going to get in touch with your

family and tell them we want a million dollars cash by tomorrow afternoon."

Rosita gasped. "A million dollars?"

Petey piped in. "He's got viewing rooms
all over New Jersey, and his wife sells a lot
of books. Hey, C.B., maybe we should ask
for more."

C.B. ignored him.

"I can guarantee my family will pay you
the money," Luke said carefully. "But it's
Thursday afternoon of Christmas weekend. I don't know how they'd be able to
get it by tomorrow."

"Believe me, they can," C.B. said. "If
they want to."

"He read it in a book," Petey volunteered. "Banks do things for important
people, like opening their doors at all
hours. And you're a real important person."

"But my wife is in the hospital," Luke
protested.

"We know that. Where do you think we
picked you up?" C.B. asked. "Now—who
do you want us to call?"

"My daughter. She just got in from California. She'll get you the money." He gave

them her cell-phone number: "310-555-4237."

Petey started scribbling the number on a piece of paper he had torn off the brown deli bag. "Say that again."

Luke repeated the number slowly.

C.B. turned the phone on and began dialing.

"That implant came out smooth as silk," Dr. Jay assured Alvirah. "I have Willy on oxygen now. I'd like you to wait a little while before you take him home. He's still groggy."

"That laughing gas really knocks Willy out," Alvirah commented. "But he sure was looking forward to it. He's been in such misery."

"Well, give him a couple of days, and he'll be good as new. The prescription for antibiotics should clear up his infection." Dr. Jay's pleasant, bespectacled face broke into a smile. "He'll be able to enjoy the Christmas holiday. I know *I'm* looking forward to it." He looked at his watch. "I have one more patient, and then I'm on vacation."

"Any big plans?" Alvirah queried with her usual genuine interest in the comings and goings of her fellow creatures.

"My wife and I are taking the kids skiing in Vermont."

"Nice," Alvirah said, shaking her head. "When we won the lottery, I made a list of all the things I've always wanted to do in this lifetime. Skiing was one of them. But I haven't gotten around to it yet."

She did not miss the alarmed expression on Dr. Jay's face. "I bet you think I couldn't do it," she challenged.

"Alvirah, I've known you long enough. Nothing you do would surprise me."

Alvirah laughed. "Don't worry. I won't crash into you on the slopes just yet. If the weather reports are right about a storm, you should have some great skiing."

"If it does hit, we'll already be there. We're leaving tonight." Dr. Jay looked at the door. "He's never late," he murmured more to himself than to Alvirah, then said, "I'll check on Willy and start to wrap things up around here."

As the doctor left the waiting room, Alvirah admitted to herself that she really had been worried about Willy—more worried than she had allowed herself to realize. Willy has always been so healthy, she thought. I won't even let myself consider that something could be seriously wrong with him. She was so deep in thought that the ringing of the office bell startled her. That must be the patient Dr. Jay is waiting for, she reasoned. She jumped up to answer the door as a buzzer released the lock.

Alvirah immediately knew that the slender, dark-haired young woman who came into the waiting room was not the patient Dr. Jay was expecting. She had clearly heard him say that *"he"* was never late.

She quickly sized up the newcomer— around thirty, very attractive, wearing a handsome suede jacket, jeans, and boots; obviously preoccupied. She smiled fleetingly at Alvirah as she looked at the empty reception desk.

"Everybody except Dr. Jay has gone home already," Alvirah volunteered cheerily. "He's waiting for his last patient."

Alvirah could see that the look of concern on the young woman's face immediately deepened.

Dr. Jay appeared at the doorway. "Hi,

Regan. Where's your father? He's holding up my vacation."

"I was hoping to hook up with him here," Regan said.

"Well, he should be along any minute. I expected him half an hour ago."

"It's so unlike my father to be late."

"There's a lot of traffic out there," Dr. Jay said with a wave of his hand.

The expression on Regan's face, however, remained clearly troubled.

"Is anything wrong?" he asked her.

Regan walked closer to the doctor and lowered her voice, a useless exercise, since Alvirah Meehan could hear a mouse sneeze from three rooms away. "It's been kind of crazy," she began, and briefly explained about her mother's accident.

That's who she is! Alvirah thought: Nora Regan Reilly's daughter. Of course! I thought she looked familiar. She's a private investigator, just like me. Only she has a license. Alvirah sat up straight and cocked her head, praying they didn't move into Dr. Jay's private office.

"I thought I'd help my father do some shopping this afternoon after he saw you," Regan was saying. "Because we were planning to go to Hawaii, we don't have a Christmas tree or any food in the house."

I love Hawaii, Alvirah thought.

"What worries me," Regan continued, "is that I can't reach my father on his cell phone, and he hasn't called my mother since he left her room at the hospital this morning. And now he isn't here. None of this is like him." Her voice was forlorn.

Uh-oh, Alvirah thought. She's right. Something's wrong.

"Well, let's wait and see," Dr. Jay said reassuringly. "He'll probably be here any minute. If he isn't, with all that happened today, it must mean that he simply forgot. He's obviously got a lot on his mind. I'm sure there's a logical explanation."

He looked over at Alvirah. "Willy should be ready to go in about fifteen minutes."

"Take your time," Alvirah said, grateful that Willy wasn't ready yet to walk out the door. She watched as Regan restlessly crossed to the window, looked out at the parking area, then sat in the straight-backed chair opposite the couch.

After a moment, Alvirah leaned forward. "I just want you to know that I've read every one of your mother's books and I love them. I was so sorry to hear about her accident. I can see you're worried about your father, but take my word, when something happens to a wife, husbands are useless. They forget everything."

Regan smiled slightly. "I hope you're right. I'm going to try calling him again." She pulled out her cell phone and dialed. "No answer," she said. "I'll try the hospital."

Let him be there or have called, Alvirah prayed as Regan spoke to her mother's nurse.

Regan put down the phone. "My mother is still asleep, which is good. My father hasn't called, which isn't." She stood up and once again walked to the window.

Alvirah wanted to say something comforting, but she knew there was nothing to be said. Had something happened to Luke Reilly?

Nearly twenty minutes later he was still not there.

"Okay, Alvirah, you can collect your patient," Dr. Jay said as he came down the hall, his hand under Willy's arm.

"Hi, honey," Willy said feebly.

"Take him home and let him sleep it off,"

Dr. Jay instructed. "And have a great holiday." He turned to Regan: "Any word?"

"Dr. Jay, I think it's obvious my father isn't going to make it today. I'll call a cab to take me to the house. I'm sure I'll catch up with him there."

"Don't you live here in Summit?" Alvirah asked, but didn't wait for an answer. "I know you do. It says so on the book jackets. We've got a car and driver outside. We'll drop you home. Come on, Willy."

Before she could protest, Regan found herself sitting next to Alvirah in the backseat of a sleek, black limo. Willy, his legs stretched out, his eyes shut, was leaning back on the opposite seat.

"I've taken driving lessons three times in the last three years," Alvirah explained. "The instructors always found excuses to pass me off on someone else." She laughed. "I can't blame them. You wouldn't believe all the parking cones I've flattened."

Regan smiled. She instinctively liked Alvirah and realized now that she had heard her name somewhere before. As the car pulled onto the main road, she said, "I feel as though I know you from some-where. Your name is familiar."

Alvirah beamed. "I know you're a private investigator, and I guess you could say I'm kind of in your business. I've accidentally been around when the police needed help. Then I've written about what happened for the *Globe.* I'm what you might call 'a roving crime correspondent.' "

"Roving isn't the word," Willy volunteered, without opening his eyes. "Alvirah's always at full throttle, looking for trouble."

Regan laughed. "My mother sent me a couple of your columns. She enjoyed them and thought I'd be interested in the cases. She was right." Alvirah's coat was open. Regan leaned over. "Is that your famous pin with the hidden microphone?"

"I never leave home without it," Alvirah said proudly.

Regan reached into her pocket. "I'm going to try my father's office."

But there was nothing new: Austin Grady still hadn't heard from Luke.

With a sigh, Regan clicked off the phone.

For the next five minutes, Alvirah did a

running commentary on the Christmas decorations of the various houses they passed. Finally Regan said, "That's our house up on the left."

"Oh, lovely," Alvirah breathed, craning her neck to get a better look. "A lot nicer than the houses I used to clean, I'll tell you that."

It was obvious that no one was home. The Reilly house, unlike its neighbors, was in total darkness.

The long driveway extended to the garages at the rear of the house. The chauffeur stopped at the walk that led to the front door.

"Let me go in with you while you check your messages, Regan," Alvirah said, a note of concern in her voice.

Regan knew what Alvirah meant. If there had been an accident, there might be a call on the machine. "I'll be fine, Alvirah. I can't thank you enough. You need to get Willy home."

Reluctantly Alvirah watched Regan go up the steps and disappear into the house. The car began to move slowly down the driveway. They were just turning back onto the street when the soft ring of a cell phone made Alvirah look around quickly. I don't have mine with me, she thought. Then she spotted it. The phone Regan had been using was on the seat next to her, its green light flashing.

I'll answer it, she thought. I bet it's her father. She picked it up and flipped it open.

"Hello," she boomed happily.

"Regan?" The voice was deep and raspy.

"I'll get her," Alvirah said, as she yelled for the driver to go back. "Is this her father?"

"It's a message from him."

"Oh, good," Alvirah shouted.

As Alvirah jumped out of the car and ran up the walk, she did not hear C.B.'s comment to Luke: "Whoever answered your daughter's phone has a voice like a foghorn."

Fred Torres hung up his uniform and closed the door of his locker with a decisive snap. "That's it for two weeks, Vince," he said to his partner. "It's anchors away for me."

"I wish I were going sailing in the Caribbean," Vince Lugano said as he pulled on a sweater. "While you're on deck with a beer in your hand, I'll be putting together a fire engine and a dollhouse."

The tiny lines around Fred's dark brown eyes crinkled when he smiled. "You love every minute of it," he said.

"I know I do," Vince agreed, looking with affection at the man who had become his best friend since they were sworn in as police officers in Hoboken, New Jersey, six years ago.

Fred was twenty-eight years old, just under six feet tall, lean and muscular. His olive complexion, dark hair, and general good looks made him the perfect target for well-meaning friends who just happened to have an available sister or cousin. He was about to begin his final term at Seton Hall Law School after the holidays.

Vince, the same age as his partner, was two inches taller and twenty pounds heavier, with sandy hair and hazel eyes. He had never been interested in anyone except his high-school sweetheart, whom he married five years ago.

"What time do you leave?" Vince asked.

"I've got an eight o'clock flight tomorrow morning."

"You'll be at Mike's party tonight?"

"Sure."

"See you there."

Fred had intended to drive straight home to his apartment in a small brownstone at the south end of town. But he impulsively stopped when he turned the corner that led to his street and spotted the dazzling array of poinsettias in the flowershop window. It won't take that long, he assured himself as he went in and selected a plant. He had met Rosita Gonzalez at a party a month ago, and they'd gone out to dinner together a couple of times since. He had invited her to the party tonight, but she didn't have anyone available to baby-sit.

As he got back in the car, he smiled, thinking of her and remembering the night they had met. They both had arrived at that party at the same time. He had parked behind her. She had been driving a glistening black limousine. As they walked up the steps together, he introduced himself and said, "You certainly arrive in style."

"Wait till you see what I go home in," Rosita had joked. "Among my activities, I drive a limo. One of the guys I work with will be dropping off my car and taking this one."

When the party ended, Fred had walked her out to her twelve-year-old Chevy. "Just call me Cinderella," she said with a smile.

She seemed so young, with her long, dark hair and infectious laugh, that it was hard for him to believe that she was the mother of two little boys.

"Does Cinderella have a phone number?" he asked.

And now, as he found himself driving to her house, Fred wondered if this was such a good idea. There was more traffic than he had expected, and he hadn't begun to pack for his trip. He admitted to himself that showing up at her house might be sending Rosita the wrong message. He had no intention of getting too involved with anyone at this point. For the foreseeable future, he wouldn't have enough time to devote to a relationship—especially one that involves kids, he thought.

Rosita lived in a modest garden-apartment complex not far from Summit. The shortest day of the year was yesterday, Fred thought. I can believe it. At 4:30 it was completely dark. He parked in a visitor's space, went up the path, shifted the festively wrapped plant to one hand, and rang the bell of Rosita's ground-floor unit.

Inside the apartment, seventeen-year-old Nicole Parma was in a state of near hysteria. At the sound of the chimes, she rushed to the door. "Your mother probably forgot her key," she yelled to Chris and Bobby, both of whom were sitting cross-legged in front of the television set.

Neither one of them looked up. "Mommy never forgets her key," six-year-old Chris said matter-of-factly to his younger brother. Only eleven months apart in age, they could pass for twins.

"But Mommy said she'd be home by now," Bobby said, his voice low and troubled. "I don't like Nicole. She won't play with us like Sarah does." Sarah was their regular baby-sitter.

Forgetting all of Rosita's warnings about not opening the door until she knew who was on the other side, Nicole flung it open. Fred did not miss her look of acute disappointment when she saw him standing there.

"Is Mrs. Gonzalez home?" He took a step back, not wanting to suggest that he would make any attempt to enter unless invited.

"No, and I expected her over an hour ago!" The answer was almost a wail.

"It's Fred!" Chris shouted, jumping up.

"Fred!" Bobby echoed.

Both boys were at the door, crowding past Nicole to greet him.

"That's Mommy's friend!" Chris told her. "He's a policeman. He arrests people."

"Hello, you two." Fred looked back at Nicole. "I just wanted to drop this plant off for the boys' mother."

The boys were pulling at Fred's jacket.

"I can tell it's all right if you come in," Nicole said. "Rosita should be here any minute."

"Mommy better be here soon," Chris volunteered as Fred stepped inside. "Nicole's freaking out. She's got to get ready for her dance tonight and doesn't want to look ugly 'cause she lovvvvves her boyfriend. Ha ha ha, Nicole."

If looks could kill, Fred thought, as the young girl glared at Chris.

"You brat! I told you to hang up the phone when I was talking before."

"Kissy, kissy, see you later, I can hardly wait." Chris made a loud smacking sound with his lips.

"Kissy, kissy," Bobby repeated, mimicking his brother's singsong tone.

"Come on, guys," Fred said. "That's enough." He saw the tears shining in Nicole's eyes. "You're running late, I guess."

"Really late," she confirmed, as her mouth quivered and the tears began to roll down her cheeks.

"Hasn't Rosita called?"

"No. I tried her cell phone, but there was no answer."

"She must be on her way home." The same impulse that had made him stop at the flower shop elicited the next words from his mouth: "Look, I've got some time. I can wait with the kids." He started to pull out his police ID. "You can see the boys know me."

Chris ran over to an end table and picked up a framed picture. It was a group shot taken at the party where Fred and his mother had met. "There he is!" he cried, pointing at the photograph and running over to Nicole. "That's him in the back row."

Nicole barely glanced at Fred's ID or at the good-times snapshot before she was out the door, one arm already in the sleeve of her coat.

"She's a pain," Chris observed. "All she did was talk on the phone with her boyfriend. Yuck."

"She wouldn't play checkers," Bobby said quietly.

"She *wouldn't?*" Fred said, his voice suitably incredulous. "I *love* to play checkers. Let's find a place to put Mommy's plant, then we'll see if you two can beat me. Red or black?"

When Regan opened the door, Alvirah waved the cell phone at her. "The call you've been waiting for!" she said breath-lessly.

Regan grabbed the phone. "Dad?"

Without hesitation, Alvirah stepped inside and closed the door. I just want to make sure everything's all right, she told herself. But an instant later, judging by the look on Regan's face, she was certain that something was very, very wrong.

Instead of the voice Regan had been expecting to hear, she was chilled by a curt command, "You'll talk to him in a minute. Get rid of whoever is with you."

This isn't the police or a hospital calling, Regan thought. She made a snap decision to let Alvirah stay. Not that she would have had much choice. Alvirah's two feet were practically glued to the marble floor. But the concern in her eyes made Regan glad for her presence. "Thank you, Alvirah," she said loudly. "I won't keep you." She reached past her and noisily opened and closed the door.

That guy doesn't want anyone else to overhear what he's telling Regan, Alvirah thought. Yanking open her coat, she quickly unhooked the sunburst pin that she always wore, turned on its tiny hidden microphone, and handed the pin to Regan.

Regan's eyes widened at first, and then she nodded, realizing what Alvirah intended. "Let me talk to my father," she said as she held the sunburst pin next to her ear and the earpiece of the phone.

"Not so fast," the gruff voice snapped. "I've got a list of demands."

In the houseboat, Petey nodded his approval. "Kind of like a top-ten list," he whispered to Luke, with a friendly punch to his manacled arm.

C.B. glared at him.

"Sorry."

C.B. continued. "You must have one million dollars in cash by tomorrow afternoon. It must be in one-hundred-dollar bills, in a duffel bag. At six o'clock on the dot, and I *mean* on the dot, be in your car driving into Central Park at the Sixth Avenue entrance. You will receive a phone call telling you where to leave the money. Do not call the police if you want to see your father and his cutie-pie chauffeur again. Once the money has been received and counted, you'll get a call about where to pick them up."

"I want to talk to my father now," Regan demanded.

C.B. walked over to Luke and held the phone to his ear. "Say hello to your little girl. And tell her she'd better do as she's told."

It was with heartsick relief that Regan heard Luke's calm voice. "Hi, Regan. We're both okay so far. Your mother will know where to get the money quickly."

Before Regan could answer, C.B. pulled the phone away. "That's enough from you. It's Rosita's turn." He was at her side. "Say hello to Regan."

The words rushed out of Rosita's mouth. "Take care of my boys."

Again C.B. didn't give Regan a chance to respond. "Okay, Regan Reilly," he said. "We've got a date. Six o'clock tomorrow. Right?"

"I'll be there," Regan said. "But I have to talk to my father and Rosita again before I drop that money." Trying to keep the mounting fury out of her voice, it was her turn to ask, "Right?"

"You've got it, Regan." The line went dead.

• • •

"Beverly, I feel like nine miles of torn-up road," Nora told her nurse as she looked into the mirror of her small compact and applied lipstick.

Beverly Carter smiled. "You look fine, Mrs. Reilly," she said reassuringly, fluffing up Nora's pillows. "I'm glad you slept so long. You seem a lot better than you did this morning."

"I certainly feel better," Nora said, glancing at her watch. "It's 6:30. Let's turn on the news and see what else has happened in the world today."

"It's me," Regan announced as she pushed open the door which had been slightly ajar.

Nora's face brightened. "You're early. That's great. Where's Dad?"

Regan hesitated. "He's been delayed."

"Mrs. Reilly, I'll be outside if you need me," the nurse said.

"Beverly, why don't you go have dinner?" Regan suggested. "We'll be visiting for a while. Take your time."

When the nurse left, Regan closed the

door and slowly turned around to face her mother. Her expression was troubled.

"Regan, what is it?" Nora asked, her voice suddenly panicky. "What's wrong? Has something happened to Dad?"

"Mom, I . . ." Regan began, searching for the right words.

"He's not dead, is he?" Please God, Nora thought, not that.

"No, no—nothing like that," Regan said swiftly. "I spoke to him a couple of hours ago."

"Then what? What is it?"

"There's no simple way to tell you. He's been kidnapped, and someone called me with a ransom demand."

"Mother of God," Nora whispered. She clasped her hands against her chest as if to shield herself from another blow. "How did it happen? What do you know?"

Regan hated to see the pain on her mother's face as she related the little she knew about Luke's disappearance: her attempts to reach him; her decision to go to Dr. Jay's office; the ride to their home in Summit with Alvirah Meehan, whose articles about crime Nora had sent to her;

and finally, the call on her cell phone de-manding the million-dollar ransom.

"If Rosita's with him, and he didn't make it to the funeral, then the kidnapping must have happened right after he left here this morning." Nora's eyes welled with tears. She looked out the window. It was impos-sible to believe her husband of thirty-five years was out there somewhere in that cold, dark night, at the mercy of someone who might at any moment snuff out his life. "We can get the million dollars. But Regan, we have to let the police in on this."

"I know. Alvirah is friendly with the guy who runs the Major Case Squad here in Manhattan. He would be the right person to call. That squad handles high-profile kidnappings. Alvirah is with me. She's waiting outside."

"Bring her in," Nora said, "but wait a minute. Who else knows about this?"

"Nobody except Alvirah's husband and his sister, who's a nun. She's staying with him right now. After the dental surgery, he's pretty out of it."

"What about Rosita's children? Who's minding them?"

"I got her phone number from Dad's Rolodex," Regan replied. "When I called, I spoke to a friend of hers who said he had just relieved the baby-sitter. I only told him that Rosita had been detained, but I could tell that he suspects something is seriously wrong."

"As long as the kids are all right for the moment." Nora took a deep breath as she tried to pull herself up on the bed. Damn this leg, she thought. To be trapped like this when every fiber of her being screamed for her to take some action. "Let's get Alvirah in here," she said. "We'll get in touch with her connection in the police department and then get a million dollars together."

Regan had scarcely opened the door before Alvirah bustled into the room, walked over to the bed, and gave Nora Reilly's hand a reassuring squeeze. "We're going to get your husband and that girl back safe and sound," she promised.

There was something about Alvirah Meehan that made Nora believe she could do just that.

"Last year I lectured at John Jay College about the case of a baby whose kidnapping I solved," Alvirah told her. "The newspapers called it the baby bunting case because I found the bunting the baby had been wearing when she was abducted from the hospital."

"I remember that case," Nora said. "That one was right around Christmas too."

Alvirah nodded. "Yes, it was. We got the baby back on Christmas Eve. Jack Reilly was at my lecture that day and invited me to have lunch with him. He's the grandest fellow, and so smart. Only thirty-four years old and already in charge of the Major Case Squad with the rank of captain." She reached for the phone. "He'll know how to handle this. He works out of One Police Plaza."

"Reilly?" Nora asked.

"Can you believe that? And he spells it just like you do too. I asked him that day if you were related." Alvirah waved her hand dismissively. "You're not."

Regan smiled slightly as she sat on the edge of the bed and closed her hand over her mother's outstretched fingers. Together they listened to Alvirah's refusal to take no for an answer.

"I don't care if he's not due back until Monday," Alvirah was saying. "Nobody else will do. I want you to page him now. Here's the message: 'It is absolutely urgent that you call Alvirah Meehan immediately at . . .' what's the phone number here, Regan?"

"Give him my cell-phone number," Regan replied. "It's 310-555-4237."

Alvirah replaced the receiver. "Knowing Jack Reilly, I'll hear from him in the next ten minutes."

Eight minutes later the cell phone rang.

Jack Reilly did not even mind the particularly impossible traffic on the East River Drive. His suitcase was in the trunk, and he was headed for his parents' house in Bedford. It was evident that the usual one-hour trip would take almost double that time tonight. The holiday exodus from Manhattan was well under way.

Of his six siblings, he hadn't seen two of his brothers and one of his sisters since August, when they'd all been at the family home on Martha's Vineyard. Counting spouses and children, there'd be nineteen of them under the same roof for the next four days. I just hope we don't end up killing each other, he thought with a grin. The weather reports were indicating a heavy storm over the weekend.

He jammed on the brake. Despite the bumper-to-bumper traffic, the car on his right had made a sudden move and cut in front of him. "You'll get there a lot faster now, won't you pal?" he muttered, looking out at the mass of red taillights that extended as far as the eye could see.

Jack Reilly had sandy hair that tended to curl, hazel eyes more green than brown, even features with a strong jaw, and a broad-shouldered, six-foot-two body. Keenly intelligent, quick-witted, and with a sharp sense of humor honed by growing up in a large family, he had undeniable charisma. Both at social gatherings and at work, his laid-back presence somehow filled the room.

His easygoing manner disappeared, however, when he was on a case. The grandson of a New York police lieutenant, after graduating from Boston College he surprised his family by making the decision to pursue a career in law enforcement. In the twelve years that followed, he had risen through the ranks from patrolman to captain and head of the Major Case Squad. Along the way he also had picked up two master's degrees. His goal was to become police commissioner of New York, and few who knew him doubted he would make it.

His pager beeped. He had taken it off and laid it in the well of the car's console. He picked it up, glanced at the number, and was not at all happy to see that it was his office trying to reach him. Now what? he thought as he pulled out his cell phone.

Fifteen minutes later he was tapping on the door of Nora's hospital room. Alvirah ran over to open it. "I'm so glad you got here so fast!" she exclaimed.

"I was right by an exit on the FDR Drive," Jack said as he greeted Alvirah with a peck on the cheek. He looked past her and recognized the face of Nora Regan Reilly. He knew the very attractive young woman standing beside her had to be her daughter. He had seen that same anguished expression on the faces of the relatives of other kidnap victims. They wanted help, not sympathy.

"I'm Jack Reilly," he said as he shook hands with both of them. "I'm terribly sorry about what's happened. I know you want to get right down to business."

"Just the facts, ma'am," Regan said with a ghost of a smile. "Yes, we do."

I like him, Nora thought as he took out a notebook. He's solid. He knows what he's doing. With a pang, she watched Jack Reilly glance around and pull up the chair Luke had occupied that very morning.

Immediately after they made the phone call to Regan Reilly, C.B. and Petey put on their coats and hats. As C.B. gratuitously explained to Luke and Rosita, it was happy hour at the bar in Edgewater at which he had met Petey some months earlier.

"Yeah," Petey brayed. "And wouldn't ya know, Mr. Reilly, we met because of you."

"How did I manage that?" Luke asked, an edge in his voice as he flexed his fingers and shifted the handcuffs to move them past his wrist bones.

"I'll tell ya. Talk about coincidence. A couple of weeks after I painted your viewing room, I'm sitting at Elsie's Hideaway, and there's C.B., sitting at the other end of the bar, drowning his many sorrows."

"You were in a pretty sorry state yourself," C.B. interjected.

"Yeah," Petey agreed. "I gotta admit. At the time I wasn't feeling so good about life myself."

"Losers," Rosita muttered under her breath.

"Huh?" Petey asked.

"Nothing."

"Come on, Petey," C.B. said impatiently. "Let's go. The cheese and crackers will be gone before we get there."

"The crowd that place attracts—vultures, every one of them," Petey said, shaking his head with disgust. Hellbent on finishing his story, he continued: "So I said to myself, I've seen that guy before. But where? Then I said to myself, wowie—I know where. It was at that lively joint of yours, Mr. Reilly. Turns out he and that old buzzard of an uncle had stopped by while I was doing the paint job."

"What a beautiful story," Rosita said sarcastically.

"Yeah. So I bring my beer over, friendly

like, and we got to talking." Petey's voice changed. "And he told me you were all making jokes about that nice color I painted your room—and after I'd mixed it special for you."

C.B. opened the door to the deck. "When Uncle Cuthbert took a look at that room, he said he'd rather be waked in a fun house."

"That really hurt my feelings," Petey lamented. "But it all worked out for the best." His face brightened. "If he and his uncle hadn't poked their noses into the room, I wouldn't have met C.B. And now we're gonna start a new life with your million dollars, Mr. Reilly. We'll be on the beach, meeting gorgeous girls and everything."

"Good for you," Luke snapped. "Does that radio over there work?" He nodded his head in the direction of the little kitchen.

Petey glanced at the top of the refrigerator where a scratched and painfully old radio was perched precariously. "Sometimes. If the batteries are working." He reached up and flipped it on. "What's your fancy? News or music?"

"News," Luke said.

"There'd better be no bulletin about your disappearance," C.B. said darkly.

"I assure you there won't be."

Petey twisted the dial until he found an all-news station. The sound was raspy and tinny, but clear enough to be understood. "Enjoy," he said as he followed C.B. out the door.

After they left, Luke and Rosita listened to the traffic and weather reports. A nor'easter was making its way up the East Coast. According to the forecast, it would be in Washington, D.C., tomorrow and was expected to hit the New York area on Christmas Eve.

"Listen up, you last-minute shoppers," the announcer cautioned. "We expect between eight and ten inches of snow, high winds, and icy road conditions. So it would be wise to get all your shopping completed by tomorrow afternoon. On Saturday the roads are going to be hazardous, so play it safe and make plans to stay home by the tree."

"I was going to put up our tree tonight, with my sons," Rosita said quietly. "Mr.

Reilly, do you think we'll be home on Christmas Eve?"

"Nora and Regan will make sure that the money is paid. And I really do believe these guys intend to let us go. Or at least they'll tell someone where to find us once they have the money in their hands."

Luke did not tell Rosita what was now becoming his greatest fear. Stupid as they were, C.B. and Petey would never disclose his and Rosita's whereabouts until they were safely beyond the long arm of the law. This probably meant they'd be heading to a country that would not extradite them. If we're still here on Saturday, Luke thought, this river might be loaded with chunks of ice that could easily tear holes in this rotting tub. It had already been an unusually cold December. A storm would pull the ice that had already formed up north down the river.

Three long hours later, C.B. and Petey reappeared, this time carrying bags from McDonald's.

"Elsie put out some spread," Petey rejoiced. "Normally, she's a Scrooge, but I guess miracles happen during the holidays. Although she did get annoyed when I tried to fix a little doggie bag for you two. That's why we picked up some Big Macs."

"Set it out for them," C.B. ordered. "Then get blankets and pillows from the bedroom. As soon as they eat and get settled for the night, I'm out of here. And you get a good night's sleep too, Petey. We've got a big day tomorrow."

"We sure do," Petey said, his speech slightly slurred thanks to Elsie's eggnog. *"Who Wants to Be a Millionaire?* We do! C.B. and Petey, New Jersey's finest! But who needs Regis? We've got Luke Reilly."

The length of the chains made it possible for them to lie back, Luke on the banquette and Rosita across the way on the couch. For hours Luke lay awake. Petey's tumultuous snoring from the tiny bedroom reverberated through the drafty cabin, but somehow it was easier to take than the sound of Rosita crying softly in her sleep.

"I think we're all agreed," Jack Reilly said, summing up the hour they had been together in Nora's room. "Mrs. Reilly . . ." he began.

"Nora," she corrected. Maybe someday Mom, she thought with a quick flash of humor. Oh God, I can just imagine what Luke would say if I told him that in the middle of his kidnapping, I'm trying, as usual, to fix Regan up. *When* I tell him, not *if,* she corrected herself. But one thing was certain: Luke would like Jack Reilly.

"Nora," he continued. "We've canceled your private nurses. You might be getting phone calls here about Luke and Rosita, and the fewer people who know about this, the better. Now I want you to try and get some rest. If you think of anyone who might hold a grudge, for whatever reason, against you or Luke, or even Regan, call me immediately."

Nora shook her head and raised her hands helplessly. "I just can't imagine."

"I understand. Of course, we'll be checking into Rosita's ex-husband as well," he said, then paused. "And then again, this could just be someone who knows that you have money."

"That's why when the lottery commission asked me and Willy to do a commercial about how happy we are with all our money, I told them to go jump in a lake," Alvirah announced. "Of course, I'd already been on plenty of shows, but enough's enough."

"You're right, Alvirah," Jack assured her. "Nora, first thing in the morning, you'll contact your broker and arrange a million-dollar loan against your stock portfolio. You're sure they won't start asking questions?"

"It's our money," she said firmly. "Nobody tells us what to do with it."

Regan was glad to see that her mother's fighting spirit was returning.

"We'll alert the Federal Reserve bank to start assembling the ransom money," Jack said. Then he turned to Regan. "You and Alvirah are going to Rosita's home now to speak with whomever is baby-sitting her sons. You'll have to use your discretion about how much to tell him. Our people should have her phone covered by now. If this baby-sitter wants to leave, we can send a social worker over."

"I have the perfect person for the job," Alvirah said triumphantly. "Sister Maeve Marie. She works with Cordelia, Willy's sister. Maeve's great with kids, and she used to be on the New York City police force. And like Sister Cordelia, she can make the Sphinx look like a blabber-mouth."

Jack smiled. "Good. And Regan, after checking out Rosita's home situation, you and Alvirah are going to meet your father's assistant at his office."

Regan nodded. At Jack's request, she had phoned Austin Grady and obtained the license number of the car Rosita had been driving, as well as the E-Z Pass account number. Jack had already called this information in to his office.

They had agreed that Austin had to be fully informed, but the only thing Regan had told him so far was that there was a serious problem. "He'll be waiting there for us," she said.

"You'll bring the car you'll be driving for the ransom drop back into the city tonight," Jack confirmed.

"Yes. My mother's BMW."

"One of my guys will meet you later at your parents' apartment on Central Park South. He'll take the car downtown to be bird-dogged."

All three women knew "bird-dogging" was the slang for placing an electronic device attached by a magnet under the car so it could be tracked by a helicopter. Another tracking device would be placed with the ransom money, so that once it was transferred, the money could be followed to wherever the kidnappers were taking it.

The hope, of course, was that the kidnappers would then lead them to where the hostages were being kept.

"Alvirah, let me have the recording you made of the ransom call," Jack said.

"I want a copy of it first thing in the morning," Alvirah ordered as she unsnapped the cassette from the back of her sunburst pin.

"Another brilliant move by Alvirah," Jack said with affection, holding up the tiny cassette. "Even if he tried to disguise it, we have the kidnapper's voice on tape, and our tech guys may be able to learn something from the background sounds."

As Alvirah beamed at him, he kissed her cheek. "My team will be waiting for me down at One Police Plaza." He touched Nora's hand. "Try not to worry too much."

He turned to Regan. "We'll keep each other posted."

When he left, the room suddenly felt empty. There was a momentary pause, and then it was as though the three women had the same thought at once.

There was no time to waste.

It had been a busy day for Ernest Bumbles, president and chairman of the board of the Seed-Plant-Bloom-and-Blossom Society of the Garden State of New Jersey. He awoke in the morning to the happy realization that it wasn't all just a dream. Cuthbert Boniface Goodloe had indeed left virtually his entire estate to the society.

The joyous news had reached them only hours after dear Mr. Goodloe had breathed his last. Ernest had received a call from Goodloe's lawyer with "sad news and glad news," as he put it. "Mr. Goodloe is no longer with us," he said with a sigh, "but his association with the Blossoms gave him so much pleasure for the past three years that he has left virtually his entire estate of a bit over one million dollars to your society."

Ernest had been busy mulching his thistles in the greenhouse behind his home when his wife, Dolly, had come running out with the portable phone. A sufferer of severe allergies, she covered her face with a surgical mask whenever she entered the greenhouse.

"Bumby," she cried, her voice muffled, "a call for you. He sounds smart, so it must be important. A-choo."

Even with the mask, the mulch always got to her.

The reason Mr. Withers had phoned before Goodloe had finished knocking on the pearly gates soon became clear. It had been Mr. Goodloe's express wish that the Blossoms turn out in full force for his wake, his funeral, and the luncheon to follow. Needless to say, Blossoms all across the state had dropped their shovels, ripped off their gardening gloves, and gathered to mourn their now beloved benefactor.

In the emergency board of directors meeting called by Ernest before the services, one of the members pointed out that were it not for Luke Reilly, none of this would have happened. Three years earlier, Reilly had been feted as Man of the Year at their annual banquet, in recognition of the fact that his three funeral homes were a boon to the local floral industry. The night of the award, Cuthbert Boniface Goodloe had been his guest at one of the tables Luke had been strongly encouraged to buy.

Goodloe had been so enchanted by the society's four-minute film on the positive effects of talking to your plants that he had signed up to become a member that very night.

At the meeting after Goodloe's death, they had unanimously voted that in recognition of Luke Reilly's networking skills, he would be presented a Blossom Society Proclamation at the postfuneral luncheon. Much to their disappointment, however, Reilly did not show up. His associate, Austin Grady, had informed them of Luke's wife's unfortunate accident.

Ernest was especially disappointed. He had wanted to put the framed proclamation—inscribed on the finest parchment money could buy and surrounded by dried flowers—in Luke's hands personally. He had looked forward with great anticipation to seeing the thrilled expression on his face when he unwrapped the proclamation and read the message.

TO ALL WHO READ THESE WORDS

Greetings and Salutations.
Be It Known That Luke Reilly,
By Virtue of Bringing Our Beloved
Benefactor Cuthbert Boniface Goodloe
Into the Fold of the Blossoms,
Is now and forever,
By the Authority and
Recommendation of the
Board of Directors,
Freely and Without Reservation,
A Lifelong Member of the
Seed-Plant-Bloom-and-Blossom
Society of the Garden State of
New Jersey
With all its honors, rights and
privileges thereof.
Presented on this Twenty-second
Day of December, at the dawn of the
Second Millennium,
E Pluribus Unum

When he had not appeared at the luncheon, Grady had assured Ernest that Reilly undoubtedly would drop by the funeral parlor sometime in the late afternoon. Ernest went there at five, but still there was no sign of him. Grady urged him to leave the festively wrapped gift, but that was absolutely out of the question. There are few times in one's life, Ernest thought, when you get to see pure, unadulterated joy on the face of one's fellow man. If it was humanly possible to see Luke Reilly before he and Dolly left for her mother's house on Christmas Eve and to give him that gift in person, he was going to do it.

"Bumby," Dolly said as she poured him a second cup of coffee, "if you want to stop by the funeral parlor before we go caroling with my choral group, we have to hurry."

"You're right, as usual." He gulped down the coffee and pushed back his chair.

Twenty minutes later he was back in the office of the funeral parlor inquiring about Luke Reilly's whereabouts.

"I'm afraid he's been delayed," Austin Grady said.

Bumbles thought he detected a slight irritation in the other man's voice. He was tempted to explain the contents of the package, but to do so would risk spoiling the surprise.

"I'll be back," he promised.

"We close at nine," Grady warned. "That's only a little over an hour from now."

"Tomorrow morning then," Bumbles said cheerfully as he carefully picked up the package he had rested on a chair and disappeared out the door, fragments of the proclamation running through his head. ". . . Be it known that Luke Reilly, by virtue of bringing our beloved benefactor Cuthbert Boniface Goodloe into the fold of the Blossoms . . ."

Bumbles couldn't wait until the whole world knew just what Luke Reilly had done for them.

It was 9:30 in the evening when their car pulled up to the garden apartment complex where Rosita lived. Between them, Alvirah and Regan had worked out the scenario they would follow once inside.

They needed to size up the man who was with the children. If he turned out to be very close to Rosita, they would tell him what had happened. If he was simply helping out till she got home, they would tell him they had Sister Maeve Marie ready to jump in a car and drive over from New York.

Nora had told them that Rosita's mother was now living in San Juan with the rest of her family. Jack warned that it would be unwise to notify any of them yet. "They can't do anything to help," he pointed out, "and it could create a terrible problem if word of this got out."

"Be careful," the driver warned as he opened the door and offered his hand to help Alvirah out. "It's pretty slippery here."

"He's such a nice man," Alvirah said to Regan as they walked up the path. "I felt funny when I pushed the button that raised the partition in the car so he couldn't hear us."

"So did I," Regan said. "That's why I'm glad we're picking up my mother's car right after we leave here. We've got to be able to talk freely if Jack Reilly or anyone else calls."

Alvirah knew that by "anyone else," Regan meant the kidnappers.

The driver was right; there were patches of ice on the path. Regan tucked her arm under Alvirah's elbow to keep her from slipping.

At the entrance to Rosita's ground-floor apartment, they looked at each other for a moment, then Alvirah pressed her finger firmly on the bell.

Inside, Fred was sitting on the couch, a sleepy little boy on either side of him. Hearing the bell, Chris sat up. "Maybe Mommy did forget her key," he said in a tired, hopeful voice.

Bobby rubbed his eyes as he straightened up. "Is Mommy home?"

Fred felt his throat tighten. How many times in his job had he been the one to ring the bell, bearing news of an accident or worse? Regan Reilly had been evasive on the phone. Was that what she was coming to tell them?

He experienced a fleeting instant of profound relief when he opened the door and realized there were two figures standing outside in the dark. The relief, however, was painfully short-lived. An older woman was standing next to the one he knew had to be Reilly. Perhaps a social worker, he thought with a sinking heart. If so, that means something terrible has happened to Rosita.

"Fred Torres?" the younger woman asked.

He nodded.

"I'm Regan Reilly."

"And I'm Alvirah Meehan," Alvirah said heartily.

"Come in," Fred said quietly.

Alvirah preceded Regan. She glanced around the room. Two little boys with dark hair were standing together by the couch, the expression in both sets of large brown eyes apprehensive and disappointed.

"Now which one of you is Chris and which one is Bobby?" she asked, a warm smile brightening her face. "Let me guess. Mrs. Reilly told me all about you. Chris is the oldest, so that must be you." She pointed to the taller of the two.

Chris smiled tentatively.

"I'm Bobby," the younger one said, moving closer to his brother.

"Where's Mommy?" Chris asked.

"Did you know that Mrs. Reilly broke her

leg last night?" Alvirah asked, dropping her voice as though she were telling an important secret.

"Mommy told us this morning before she left," Bobby said with a yawn. "Mommy said that tonight we would make a card and send it to Mrs. Reilly."

"Well, Mrs. Reilly needs your mommy's help tonight," Alvirah said softly. "So she just wants you two to go to bed, and she'll be home as soon as she can."

"I want her to come home now," Bobby said, suddenly on the verge of tears.

"Mrs. Reilly is nice," Chris told him. "It's all right if Mommy stays with her when she's sick."

"But when do we get to decorate our tree?" Bobby asked plaintively.

"In plenty of time for Christmas," Alvirah assured them.

Regan had been watching. Alvirah knows exactly how to handle the kids, she thought. Walking over to them, she said, "I'm Mrs. Reilly's daughter, and I'm so glad your mommy is with my mother right now. Having your mommy there makes mine feel so much better."

"Then your daddy is Mr. Reilly," Chris said. "I like his cars."

"Especially the reeeealy long ones," Bobby added, yawning again.

"You know, I think both you boys look pretty tired," Alvirah observed, "and that's just the way I feel too."

Fred knew exactly what these two women were doing—they were reassuring the boys about their mother, then they wanted them out of earshot.

"Okay, guys, bedtime," he said, putting his hands around two small shoulders.

Bobby peered up at him anxiously. "You're not going to leave us, are you Fred?"

Fred bent down and looked into the two distressed faces. He hesitated, then said firmly, "Not until Mommy gets home."

While he was settling the boys in their room, Alvirah went into the tiny kitchen and put the kettle on the stove. "I need a cup of tea," she announced. "How about you, Regan?"

"Good idea. I'd love one." Regan glanced around the cozy yet slightly cluttered apartment. The brightly slipcovered couch and matching chair with their rounded arms and thick pillows looked wonderfully comfortable. A corner with shelves had been turned over to the children's videotapes and toys. But it was the sight of the Christmas tree, already in the stand, just waiting to be decorated, that clutched at her heart.

By the time the kettle began to whistle, Fred Torres had emerged from the boys' bedroom. "I promise I'll be right out here, guys," he said as he closed the door.

Alvirah poked her head out of the kitchen. "I'm making myself at home, Fred. A cup of tea?"

"Yes, thanks." He looked at Regan. "Tell me what's going on."

"What is your relationship to Rosita?" she asked.

"We've had a couple of dates." He pulled out his police ID. "I'm a cop. Rosita's in trouble. What is it?"

Alvirah came into the living room holding a tray. "I'll put it right here on the table. Why don't we all sit down?"

Fred sat straight backed on the edge of the club chair, Alvirah and Regan opposite him on the couch.

"Fred is a police officer, Alvirah," Regan

said, then looked directly at him. "Rosita and my father were kidnapped sometime this morning. We believe it must have happened between ten o'clock, when my father left the hospital after visiting my mother, and twelve o'clock, when he was supposed to show up for a funeral."

She looked down at the cup she was holding. "At about 4:30, I received a ransom call demanding one million dollars by tomorrow afternoon. We've already met with the head of the Major Case Squad in New York."

Fred felt as though he had been punched in the stomach. "Kidnapped?" he said, his tone disbelieving, his face registering shock. He glanced down the hall at the closed bedroom door. "Those poor kids."

Alvirah turned to Fred and put her hand on the sunburst pin on her suit jacket; on the drive out to Rosita's apartment, she had inserted a new cassette. "Fred, do you mind if I record our conversation? Sometimes we say things that don't seem significant at the moment, but that really turn out to be significant later. In some cases I have worked on, listening to the tapes over and over has led to the break we needed."

"Go ahead," he said. Ignoring the cup of tea cooling in front of him, he listened intently while Regan and Alvirah filled him in on everything they knew.

"Do they have any idea who could have done this?" he asked.

"None at all," Regan said. "We think this is just about money, though. My father has no enemies that we know of."

"Did Rosita discuss her ex-husband with you?" Alvirah asked. "From what Nora told us, he's something of a ne'er-do-well who could probably use some money."

"I only met Rosita last month, at a party. We've been out to dinner twice. She didn't want to talk about him. Today the kids told me they hadn't seen him in a long time."

"He sounds like a real charmer," Regan said. "The police are going to be checking him out very carefully."

Fred shook his head. "I hope for the kids' sake he's not involved. Rosita didn't give any indication that she'd had any trouble with him lately. When we went to dinner, we talked about the usual things.

She really likes her job." He nodded at Regan. "She said your father is the best boss anyone could have. And that he keeps his cool no matter what happens. But there was nothing she said that would indicate he was having any real problem with anyone."

Regan put down her cup. "When we leave here, Alvirah and I are going over to my father's office to meet with his associate. We're going to dig around to see if perhaps there are any business problems that could be relevant. It's possible the kidnapper is a disgruntled person, perhaps even a former employee, who has a grudge against my father."

"That's sensible, and it's almost the only thing you can do. The hardest part of a kidnapping is having to wait for the kidnappers to make the next move," Fred added angrily.

"I have to keep busy," Regan said matter-of-factly, as she and Alvirah got up.

"My sister-in-law is a nun," Alvirah told Fred as she gathered the cups. "There's a young woman in her convent, Sister Maeve Marie, who was a cop before she realized she had a vocation. Maeve is wonderful with kids; she can be here in an hour if you want to go home."

Fred thought about the party he was missing, the plane he was supposed to catch in the morning, the long-planned sail with his friends. All those things seemed so trivial now. He thought about Rosita, her dark hair spilling on her shoulders, her warm smile as she joked. "Just call me Cinderella."

Not every kidnapping ended happily, he thought. In fact, many did not.

He shook his head. "You heard me tell the boys—I'm not leaving."

It had been said of Alvin Luck that his name didn't suit him. Fifty-two years old, with thinning brown hair, a slight frame, and an amiable but timid smile, he lived with his mother in a rent-controlled apartment on Manhattan's West Eighty-sixth Street. The author of twelve unpublished suspense novels, he eked out a living doing temporary jobs while waiting for his break in the publishing world.

Given the season, his current odd job was to don a red suit and white beard and ho-ho-ho his way through the toy section of a discount department store near Herald Square.

"Stop slouching, Alvin!" his boss screamed at him regularly. "Santa Claus is supposed to have some authority."

You'd think I was working for F. A. O. Schwarz and not this junk shop, he often thought.

Alvin was not without spirit.

Nor was his lack of success in the publishing world due to a lack of diligent research. He had dissected every mystery and suspense novel that had appeared on the *New York Times* bestseller list in the last twenty years, and then some. He was a virtual walking encyclopedia when it came to the plots, characters, and settings used by hundreds of suspense and mystery novelists. He had filled notebooks with plotlines, and he consulted them regularly when working on his own stories. He had divided the plots into categories such as espionage, bank robberies, murder, extortion, domestic crime, hijackings, arson, courtroom drama, and kidnapping.

His only luxury was to attend writing seminars and mystery conventions, where he listened attentively to the sage advice of published writers and later tried to corner editors at the cocktail parties.

He had been getting ready for work on Thursday when he heard on the radio the news about Nora Regan Reilly's broken leg. Over the oatmeal that his mother prepared for him every morning, he had discussed it with her.

"Mark my words," he said. "Nora's next book will be set in a hospital. She'll make the best of this situation."

"Eat your oatmeal. It's getting cold," his mother admonished.

Dutifully, Alvin picked up his spoon and slurped the somewhat lumpy mixture. "I think I'll send her a card."

"Why not stick in the picture you took of that husband of hers at the last mystery-writers' dinner?"

"You're right. I did get a good shot of him," Alvin recalled. "But only one. In the other picture his head got cut off because he's so tall."

"I like tall men. Your father was a shrimp, God rest him."

"Maybe I'll put the picture in a little holiday frame and drop it off at the hospital after work. The store has some frames with nice Christmas sayings on them."

"Don't spend too much on it," his mother cautioned.

"They're on sale," Alvin said, a trace of irritation in his voice. "Nora Regan Reilly always talks to me at the cocktail parties and is so encouraging."

"Not like those editors," his mother had sighed.

Alvin went to work, looking forward to the surprise he was planning for Nora Regan Reilly. To his disappointment, most of the best Christmas frames already had been snapped up. He settled on one that said, I'LL BE HOME FOR CHRISTMAS . . . IF ONLY IN MY DREAMS. Considering how she's stuck in the hospital, it applies more to her than to her husband, he thought, but it will have to do.

To his disgust, there was no employee discount on sale items.

"What do you expect?" the salesgirl asked as she popped her bubble gum. "They're practically giving this stuff away." She studied the frame before placing it in a bag. "Maybe that's not such a bad idea," she mumbled as Alvin carefully placed his wallet back in a deep pocket of the Santa Claus suit.

The evening-shift Santa Claus apparently had not made it down from the North Pole, and Alvin's boss told him he had to work until 8:00 P.M. That was when the sign went up that Santa was back in his workshop. By then, Alvin's ears were numb. He'd had enough of listening to the incessant demands hurled at him by an unending stream of children, all of whom seemed to take sadistic pleasure in plunking down on his boney knees.

"You don't look much like Santa," a number of the little darlings had said accusingly.

In all, it had been a long day, but that did not deter Alvin from making his planned pilgrimage to the Upper East Side. Since it was his responsibility to keep the Santa Claus suit pressed, he carried it back and forth to work. It was now neatly folded in a shopping bag, with the gift-wrapped, framed picture of Luke Reilly resting on top.

He had picked out a get-well card and written in it, "Nora, thought you'd like to have a pic of your sweetie." On a whim he signed it, "Your number-one fan."

Now he would have something to talk about with Nora Regan Reilly next time he saw her at a mystery-writers' event. He could reveal himself as the mysterious benefactor who'd sent her the nice framed picture.

Once inside the lobby of the hospital, Alvin noticed a gift shop, and in the shop window the word SALE caught his eye. Underneath the sign were perched adorable teddy bears wearing Christmas hats. He hurried in just as the shop was about to close. I won't tell Mother, he thought. But wouldn't it make it really special if a teddy bear is holding Luke Reilly's picture?

The saleswoman obligingly waited while he unwrapped the frame and stuck it in the arms of the teddy bear he had selected. She tied a huge Christmas bow around the box while Alvin counted out the exact change, which came to fourteen dollars and ninety-two cents.

Thanking her, he left the shop and went over to the reception desk. They assured him the package would go up to Mrs. Reilly immediately.

"Oh no, not until the morning," he said firmly. "I wouldn't want to disturb her. It's late."

"That's very thoughtful," the woman said pleasantly. "Have a nice holiday."

Alvin went out into the cold night air once again and walked up York Avenue to Eighty-sixth Street, to catch the crosstown bus. Glowing with Christmas spirit, he smiled cheerily at the passersby who were spilling out of restaurants and shops.

They all ignored him.

Jack Reilly's top assistant, Sgt. Keith Waters, as well as Lt. Gabe Klein, the head of TARU, the Technical Assistance Response Unit, were waiting in Reilly's office at One Police Plaza when he arrived there.

"Long time no see," Waters said laconically. "You just can't stand being away from here, can you?" A handsome black man in his late thirties, with keen intelligent eyes, he radiated restless energy.

"It's you I miss," Jack said.

But the note of levity disappeared as they promptly got down to business.

"What have you got on the car?" Jack asked.

Gabe Klein began, "The records from E-Z Pass show that the car went through the Lincoln Tunnel into Manhattan at 9:15 A.M. That would be when the girl went in to pick up Luke Reilly at the hospital. At some point the car must have been driven back to New Jersey, because it crossed the George Washington Bridge into New York again at 11:16 A.M. Then it crossed the Triborough Bridge in a lane headed for Queens at 11:45 A.M. That was the last time the E-Z Pass registered any activity."

"That means they may have reached New Jersey before they were abducted," Jack said. "Or maybe they were abducted in New York and taken to New Jersey. Most likely the car has been dumped somewhere. Stretch limos aren't that easy to hide."

"We have a bulletin out for it," Keith responded, "but nothing's turned up so far."

"You put on a safeguard for prints?"

It was a rhetorical question. That was the first thing Keith would do in a kidnapping situation. If located, the car would not be touched until the lab technicians got there.

Now, in terse sentences, Jack filled them in on the rest of the details.

Both men made notes as they listened.

Gabe Klein, fiftyish and balding, wore glasses that perched precariously on the end of his nose, giving him a bookish, slightly vague appearance. To a casual observer, he looked like the kind of man who was unable to change a lightbulb.

It was an impression that was absolutely wrong—Gabe was a technical wizard and ran the highly sophisticated unit that had become a vital tool in the police force's crime-solving efforts.

"These are the phone lines we're covering, right?" Gabe rattled off the numbers Jack had phoned in. The Reilly home and apartment, Rosita Gonzalez's apartment, the funeral homes, Nora Reilly's hospital room.

"And if they call back on the daughter's cell phone, she knows enough to try and keep them on the line so we can pinpoint the location," Gabe confirmed.

"Regan is a private investigator in Los Angeles," Jack said. "She knows the drill."

"That's a break," Keith observed. "Then you think it's okay to have her drive the car to the ransom drop?"

"She's smart," Jack said shortly. And very attractive, he thought.

"When do we get to work on the car she'll be driving?" Gabe asked.

"She's bringing it in tonight. She knows we have to birddog it."

"We've alerted the Federal Reserve that we need the million by tomorrow afternoon. They're working on it," Keith informed Jack. "Does the family have any idea who might have done this?"

"Reilly's wife and daughter can't come up with anyone. Rosita Gonzalez has an ex-husband who's something of a troublemaker. His name is Ramon. Mrs. Reilly thinks he lives in Bayonne."

"We'll get on that," Keith said.

"Rosita has two little kids. Regan Reilly is going there now to check on them and to get a fix on whoever is with them. Then she's headed to her father's office to talk to his associate."

Jack looked at his watch. "It's a long story, but Regan met Alvirah Meehan today, and now she's involved as well. Remember her? She's the lottery winner who lectured at John Jay."

"Sure I do," Keith said. "She was the one who got that baby back when all the cops in New York couldn't find her."

Jack pulled the cassette from his pocket. "Well, she's still on the ball. She managed to record the ransom call."

Gabe stared at the tiny cassette. "You're kidding." He picked it up and held it in his hand. "Does she want a job? I could use her."

"She'll have my head if you don't make an extra copy for her. But first, let's hear this tape amplified. Maybe there'll be something in the background that will help us."

As the machine was being readied, Jack felt his frustration building. They could study the tape. They could put a tracking device with the money. They could bird-dog the car. They could look for logical suspects. But until they were following Regan's wired car to the point of contact with the kidnappers, they were mostly in a waiting game.

The phone on Jack's desk rang. He picked it up. "Jack Reilly." There was a pause. "Good work," he said decisively, then looked across the desk at Gabe and Keith. "They found the limo at Kennedy Airport."

At 9:30 that evening, Austin Grady locked the doors of the Reilly funeral home behind the last of the mourners of one-hundred-and-three-year-old Maude Gherkin, the local battle-ax. In his entire career as a mortician, he had never heard the expression, "It's a blessing," uttered more often or more fervently.

Four times since her hundredth birthday, Maude had been snatched from the jaws of death. During her final hospital stay, a homemade sign had appeared over her bed: DO NOT RESUSCITATE . . . NO MATTER WHAT. The doctors suspected it was the handiwork of her eighty-year-old son, who after Maude's fourth miraculous return from the long white tunnel, had been heard to shout, "Aw, give me a *break!*"

Austin turned out the lights in the room where Maude was now resting. He sighed. Hard as they tried, they hadn't been able to get the sour expression off her face.

"Night, night, Maude," he muttered. But the little ritual he had with the clients at closing time did not bring a smile to his lips tonight—he was much too worried about Luke and Rosita.

Since Regan had phoned some hours ago, his suspicion that they had been kidnapped had become a near certainty. Why else would Regan have needed the limousine's license plate and the E-Z Pass account number? Why else couldn't she talk to him about it on the phone?

An hour later, when Regan arrived with Alvirah Meehan in tow, his suspicions were confirmed.

"The police have arranged to have these phones tapped," Regan said. "There's just a chance the kidnappers might call here."

They were startled by a sudden knocking on the window.

"What on earth?" Austin muttered as he recognized the face of none other than Ernest Bumbles, his nose pressed against the glass, who smilingly held up the package he had been carrying earlier and waved it at them.

Austin went over and struggled to raise the window.

"Sorry to bother you," Ernest said, clearly lying. "I saw your light was on and thought maybe Mr. Reilly was back."

This time Austin did not attempt to keep the irritation out of his voice. "He's not here! If you want to leave that package, I'll see that he gets it. Better yet, his daughter will take it home for him. There she is." He pointed at Regan.

Ernest stuck his head in through the open window. "I'm so pleased to meet you. Your father is a wonderful man."

I don't believe this, Regan thought.

Alvirah had turned toward the window so the sunburst pin wouldn't miss a word.

"I'm sorry I can't come in, but my wife, Dolly, is out in the car. She's not feeling that well. We were out singing Christmas carols tonight, and she strained her throat on the final fa la la la la la la la la of 'Deck the Halls.' "

That used to be my favorite Christmas carol, Regan thought. Not anymore.

"I'll be back tomorrow. I want to give this to your father personally. Bye now." Like a game show contestant who has failed to answer the final question, Ernest vanished.

Austin shut the window with a decisive snap. "That guy is a nut case."

"Who is he?" Regan asked.

"The head of some plant society," Austin said. "They honored your father a few years ago."

"I kind of remember that," Regan said. "He's active in so many organizations that he's always being honored."

Regan realized that she was played out. There was nothing more she could accomplish here at the moment. Austin had told her that there was absolutely no one he could think of who would want to bring harm to Luke. In his memory nothing unusual had happened at any of the three Reilly funeral homes.

"We'd better get going," Regan said. "I've made arrangements to stay in my mother's hospital room tonight, and I've got to get this car to Manhattan so the police can prepare it for tomorrow. Let's talk in the morning."

"Regan, I'll get here early and start going through the records from the last few months and see if there are any problems that I didn't know about," Austin promised. "I don't think I'll find anything, but it's worth a look."

As the three of them started to leave, Alvirah noticed the discreet sign bearing Maude Gherkin's name and an arrow pointing to the room where she lay in repose.

Alvirah crossed herself. "May she rest in peace. Did you ever hear the story of the woman who was passing Frank Campbell's funeral parlor in New York and had to go to the bathroom? She stopped in there and then felt she shouldn't leave without paying her respects to somebody. So she popped into a room where there were no visitors for the poor soul in the casket, said a quick prayer, and signed the register. Turned out it was in that guy's will that anyone who showed up at his wake got ten thousand dollars."

"Alvirah, you already won the lottery," Regan said, smiling.

"And believe me, you'd be wasting your time putting your John Hancock in Maude's book," Austin told her as they stepped outside and he shut and locked the door behind them. Hold down the fort, Maude, he thought.

Friday, December 23rd

"Rise and shine everybody! Time to start our million-dollar day," Petey called out as he emerged from the bedroom, clad in striped pajamas, his toothbrush in hand. He switched on the overhead light. "This is sort of like camp, isn't it?"

Why doesn't that idiot just let us sleep? Luke thought. The last time he had looked at the illuminated dial of his watch, it had been 4:00 A.M. He had finally fallen asleep, and now he was being jolted awake for absolutely no reason. He squinted at his watch. It was 7:15.

He could feel the beginning of a dull headache. His muscles were aching from a combination of the damp, cold air and being forced to contort his body to fit on the narrow, short banquette. The increasing choppiness of the river was causing the boat to knock against the dock, increasing his overall sense of misery.

A hot shower, he thought longingly. Clean clothes. A toothbrush. The little things in life.

He looked across the cabin at Rosita. She had pulled herself up on one elbow. The strain she was feeling was clearly visible on her face. Her dark-brown eyes looked enormous, stark against the increasing pallor of her complexion.

But when their eyes met, she managed a smile and tossed her head in Petey's direction. "Your valet, Mr. Reilly?"

Before Luke could reply, there was a loud pounding on the door. "It's me, Petey," C.B. yelled impatiently. "Open up."

Petey ushered him in, taking the McDonald's bags out of his hands.

"And here comes the butler," Rosita announced softly.

"Did you remember to get me an Egg McMuffin with sausage?" Petey asked hopefully.

"Yes, you moron, I did. Get dressed. I can't stand looking at you like that. Who do you think you are, Hugh Hefner?"

"Hugh Hefner gets a lot of girls," Petey

said admiringly. "When we get that million, I'm going to go out and buy a pair of silk pajamas, just like Hef's."

"If I left it to you, we'd never get that million," C.B. sputtered as he snapped on the radio.

He looked at Luke. "I was listening to *Imus in the Morning* on the way over. He put a call through to the hospital. Your wife is going to be on in a few minutes."

Nora was a frequent guest on the Imus program. Imus must have heard about the accident and phoned her. Luke sat up and leaned forward, desperately eager to hear her voice.

C.B. was twisting the dial, searching for the station. "Here we are," he said finally.

Nora's voice came through the static. "Hello, I-Man."

"Where are the hash browns?" Petey was poking through the bags.

Luke couldn't help himself. "Shut up!" he shouted.

"All right, already," Petey said.

"Nora, we were sorry to hear about your accident," Imus said. "I fall off a horse and you trip over a rug. What gives with us?"

Nora laughed.

Luke marveled at how at ease she sounded. He knew that she was feeling exactly as he would if the situation were reversed. But she had to keep up appearances to the rest of the world until this thing was resolved.

However it's resolved, he thought darkly.

"How's the funeral director?" Imus was asking.

"He's talking about you," Petey cried. "Whattayaknow!"

"Oh, he's just great," Nora said, laughing.

"He's yachting," Petey yelled at the radio, and slapped his knee, pleased as always with his own humor.

Imus was thanking Nora for the children's books she had sent his young son. "He loves it when we read to him."

Luke had a moment of acute nostalgia, remembering how he and Nora had always read to Regan when she was little. When Nora said good-bye to Imus, Luke swallowed over the lump he could feel forming in his throat. Would he ever hear her voice again?

"Mrs. Reilly sent books to my boys for

Christmas too," Rosita told him, her voice gentle. "She told me that Regan's favorite thing when she was a child was when you read to her."

And Regan had a favorite book, Luke thought, one book she always carried over to him. *"Read me this one again, Daddy,"* she'd say as she climbed on his lap. Oh my God, he thought, as he remembered which book that was.

Luke's mind began to race. He knew that C.B. had agreed to let Regan talk to him and Rosita this afternoon before she paid the ransom. Was there any chance he could somehow communicate to her a clue as to their whereabouts? Was there any way he could let her know that from where they were being held they could see the George Washington Bridge and the quaint red lighthouse perched beneath it?

Her favorite book had been about those two famous structures. Its title was *The Little Red Lighthouse and the Great Gray Bridge.*

"Bye, I-Man."

Nora hung up the phone.

"Good job, Mom," Regan said.

Both of them had slept fitfully through the night, Regan stretched out on a cot that the nursing staff had sent in. There were times when she awoke and heard her mother's light, even breathing, a sign that she was sleeping. Several times, though, she was immediately aware that Nora was awake, and they would talk quietly in the near darkness of the hospital room until sleep overtook one of them.

At one point during the night, Nora said, "You know, Regan, they claim that at the moment you die, your whole life flashes before you. I have the oddest sensation that the same kind of thing is happening to me now, but in slow motion."

"Mom," Regan protested.

"Oh, I don't mean that I'm about to die, but I guess when someone you love is in grave danger, your mind becomes a kaleidoscope of memories. Moments ago I was thinking about the apartment Dad and I had when we were first married. It was tiny, but it was ours, and we were together. He'd go off to work, and I'd hit the typewriter. Even when I kept getting rejection slips, he never doubted for one minute that I was going to make it. When I finally sold that first short story, boy, did we celebrate."

Nora paused. "I can't imagine life without him."

It took a giant effort for Regan, who had spent most of the night reliving her own memories of her father, to say softly, "Then don't."

At 6:00 A.M., Regan got up, showered, and changed into the black jeans and sweater she had picked up at the apartment before returning to the hospital.

As she and Alvirah were driving back from New Jersey the night before, she had phoned Jack Reilly and learned that the limo had been found at Kennedy Airport. He told her it had been towed to the lab at the Police Academy garage on East Twentieth Street, where they were going over it with a fine-tooth comb, looking for clues to the identity of the kidnappers.

Regan knew from her own experience the kinds of painstaking tests they would undertake and the carefully defined procedures they would follow. They would check any unidentified fingerprints they might find against the millions of prints stored in the FBI computers. They would collect any traces of fibers or hair for analysis. She had been involved in many cases where a minuscule, seemingly innocuous object turned out to be the Rosetta stone that led to the solving of the puzzle.

Jack had also filled her in on what the E-Z Pass records revealed. ". . . which as you know isn't necessarily significant. They could have been switched to another car."

Regan looked at her mother's breakfast tray, which was virtually untouched. "Why don't you at least drink the tea?" she asked.

"Irish penicillin," Nora murmured, but she did pick up the cup.

News of her accident had resulted in a deluge of flowers from the Reillys' friends. After the first few bouquets had been placed around the room, Nora requested that the others be distributed throughout the hospital.

There was a tap on the door, and a smiling volunteer asked, "May I come in?"

She was holding a box tied with a bright Christmas ribbon.

"Of course," Nora said, attempting a smile.

"First delivery of the day," the woman said sweetly. "It was left for you last night, but the girl at the desk stuck a note on it saying it should be held until the morning. So here it is!"

Nora reached up to take the box. "Thanks so much."

"Don't mention it," the woman said. She turned to Regan. "Make sure she takes good care of that leg of hers."

"I will." Regan knew she sounded abrupt, but she was anxious to keep unnecessary people out of the room. If the kidnappers happened to call before the agreed-upon time, she wanted to be able to speak freely and to record the call with the sunburst pin Alvirah had lent her.

"I always keep a backup," Alvirah had explained as she thrust the tiny recording device into Regan's hands. "Even though the cops have your phone covered, with this you'll have your own tape of any calls that come in."

Nora was sliding the bow off the box.

"Bye, now," the volunteer smiled. She walked out leaving the door slightly ajar.

As Regan was closing it, she heard a gasp from her mother and spun around.

"Regan, look at this!" Nora cried, her voice panicked.

Regan hurried over and stared down at the now open package. Inside, nestled in the arms of a stocking-capped, fluffy brown teddy bear, was a picture of her father, wearing a tuxedo and smiling warmly. But it was the lettering around the tacky red-and-green frame that shot a cold chill through her body. I'LL BE HOME FOR CHRISTMAS, it read across the top. ... IF ONLY IN MY DREAMS, completed the sentiment at the base of the frame.

There was an envelope in the box. Regan ripped it open. On an ordinary get-well card the sender had printed: "Nora, thought you'd like to have a pic of your sweetie." It was signed, "Your number-one fan."

"Let me see that." Nora took the card out of her hand. "They're threatening us, Regan!"

"I know."

"If anything goes wrong and they don't get the money . . ." Nora whispered.

Regan had already begun dialing Jack Reilly's number.

Jack had been up all night directing the frenetic activity that was the modus operandi of the Major Case Squad when involved in a breaking case.

The lab had lifted prints from the limo, and while there were many different sets to run through their computers, so far no match had been found. A few strands of polyester black hair suggested that one of the kidnappers had been wearing a disguise. The short length of the hairs indicated a fake mustache rather than a wig. The only other discovery of possibly great significance was a few tiny flecks of paint that had been found on the limousine's floor, around the brake pedal.

Suspicion for the abduction was beginning to center on Rosita's ex-husband, Ramon Gonzalez. A check with the police in Bayonne had revealed that he was well known to them. A compulsive gambler, he was rumored to be heavily in debt to local bookies and had not been spotted recently in his usual haunts.

Of potentially vital importance was the fact that Junior, his younger brother and fellow gambler, was a sometime house-painter. They shared an apartment in a run-down, two-family house. The land-lord, who also lived in the building, said that he had not seen them in a couple of days and complained that they were be-hind in their rent.

Jack had notified the FBI and was now working in tandem with them. Besides the police helicopter, which would be tracking Regan's car, an FBI fixed-wing aircraft would be overhead, ready to follow the signals sent by the device planted in the bag with the ransom money.

Alvirah's tape recording of the call from the kidnappers had been run through an exhaustive audio analysis. The voice of the person who had made the ransom de-mand, as well as those of Luke and Rosita, could be heard clearly. The feeling was that the low and almost guttural tone of the caller was almost surely an attempt to alter his normal tones. Another man's voice could be detected in the back-ground, although it was so faint that what-ever he said had not yet been deciphered.

From analyzing the ambient sounds on the tape, they were able to ascertain that Luke and Rosita were being kept in a relatively cramped area near a body of water.

As Gabe Klein observed, "That really narrows it down—three quarters of the earth is covered with water."

Now, except for the intense manhunt for the Gonzalez brothers, the police were entering the waiting-game segment of the investigation.

Regan's call, however, changed that.

"I'm on the way," Jack told her.

Twenty minutes later, Jack was in Nora's room at the hospital.

"The logo on the box is from the gift shop downstairs," Regan told him.

"There's nothing in the picture that gives me a clue about where it was taken," Nora said. "Luke and I go to a lot of black-tie affairs."

"By the time we realized what this was, our fingerprints were already on the card and the frame," Regan said.

"Don't worry about it," Jack told them. "If there are any other fingerprints, we'll get them. Do you happen to know what time the gift shop opens?"

"I already asked," Regan said. "Nine o'clock."

"How about if you go down there and speak to them?" Jack said. "See what you can find out about who might have bought this. We have to be careful not to let anyone think this is a police investigation."

"I thought I'd tell them that the person who bought the gift forgot to sign the card, and we wanted to be able to send a thank-you note."

Jack nodded. He looked at the bouquets of flowers in the room. "Nora, there's been publicity about your accident. This could, of course, be a somewhat macabre coincidence."

"I do get a lot of mail from people who read my books," Nora acknowledged. "But isn't the sentiment on that frame too much of a coincidence?"

"Possibly," Jack admitted.

"In which case, it becomes a pretty grim threat," Nora said.

Regan was studying him. "Jack, you're leaning toward coincidence. Why?"

"Because Rosita's ex-husband is our

strongest suspect, and from what I know about his type, this kind of thing is way too subtle for him. But then again . . ."

He shrugged and looked at his watch. "It's almost nine o'clock. Regan, why don't we go down to the gift shop together and see what we can find out? Then I'll take all of this downtown and give it to the lab."

He looked at Nora. "I know how upsetting this is for you. But it could be an important break for us. There may be fingerprints that will match up with some we've found in the car. If the frame wasn't bought downstairs, we'll try to trace it to where it was purchased. Perhaps someone in the gift shop will be able to give us a description of whoever bought the teddy bear."

Clearly on the verge of tears, Nora nodded. "I understand."

Jack turned to Regan. "Let's go."

Meanwhile, on the Upper West Side, barely a mile away from the hospital, Alvin Luck was bent over his bowl of oatmeal, still glowing with pleasure at the thought of the happiness his gift must be giving to Nora Regan Reilly, perhaps at this very moment.

He had wisely not broken his resolve to keep his mother in the dark about the purchase of the teddy bear. But his wisdom only went so far.

"What do you mean you didn't sign the card?" his mother badgered as she settled heavily into the chair opposite him. "Are you crazy? What were you thinking? She could help you get published. For God's sake, her editor is Michael Korda!"

"Will Mommy be home soon?"

It was the first question Chris and Bobby asked when they opened their eyes at 7:30. At least they slept well, Fred thought as he answered, "She'll be home as soon as she can."

On the shelf in Rosita's closet he had found extra sheets and a blanket and pillow, so he had bunked on the couch. It would have been more comfortable to stretch out on top of her bed, but he had found himself unable to do that. It felt almost as though it would be an invasion of her privacy.

He knew that the deeper reason was that everything in the bedroom conveyed a sense of Rosita's presence that was haunting.

A smiling picture of her with her arms around the boys dominated the top of the small dresser. There was a faint scent of perfume—a scent she had worn when he last saw her—emanating from the atomizer on her dressing table. When he had opened the closet door to find the bedding, the first thing he saw was her white silk robe and, peeking from beneath it, a pair of satin bedroom slippers.

Cinderella, he thought with a stab of pain.

Before he had settled on the couch the night before, he'd called Josh Gaspero, the friend he'd planned to meet. "Not home," he muttered to himself as Josh's machine picked up. "Figures. He's probably over at Elaine's having a Christmas drink with the regulars." The explanation he'd left had been brief. "Delayed on a special case. I can't discuss it. I'll try and catch up with you down there in a couple of days. I've got the schedule of stops."

Now he watched as Chris and Bobby went into the bathroom and reached for their toothbrushes without being told. When they began lightly splashing water on their faces, though, Fred decided to lend a hand. "As my mother used to tell me, 'You wash for a high neck,' " he said as he rubbed soap on a warm washcloth and took over.

While he made coffee, the boys got their own cereal and juice. "Please, will you make the toast in the oven?" Chris asked. "Our toaster broke, and we're not allowed to turn on the gas ourselves."

"Mommy gets really mad if we play near the stove," Bobby volunteered.

"Mommy's right," Fred replied.

Had the lab found anything significant in the limo? he wondered. By now they would have gone over it thoroughly. Alvirah Meehan had called him from her apartment last night and told him about the find. "Regan asked me to let you know. She said we'll keep you informed on anything that comes up."

As they were finishing breakfast, Sgt.

Keith Waters from the Major Case Squad phoned. "Captain Reilly asked me to call you, Fred. I know what the situation is out there. Let me bring you up to date on what we have here."

He began with the results of the lab's inspection of the limo and the focus on Ramon Gonzalez and his brother.

"We're homing in on them. You're in place in Rosita's apartment. We want you to go through it carefully and see if you can find anything that would suggest that her ex was either threatening her or trying to get money from her. Keep your eye out for anything that would show where he might be hiding out now. You know the routine. We have a search warrant, of course."

Fred was aware that the boys were listening intently to his conversation, trying to figure out who was on the phone. "Will do," he said, "and if you see Rosita, tell her that the boys are being very good and are glad she's helping Mrs. Reilly."

"But tell her she has to be home for Christmas," Bobby cried out, dismayed.

"And ask her when we're going to decorate the tree." Now even Chris seemed to be about to cry.

"What are you going to tell them?" Waters asked softly.

"Sure, I'll be glad to," Fred replied heartily. He turned to the boys. "Mommy sent word that she's going to be really tired when she gets home, so she'd like it a lot if we'd decorate the tree for her today."

He saw the doubtful look on their faces. "I'm really good with the lights, and I can reach to the top. We'll save your favorite ornaments for your mom to hang when she gets home. How about that?"

"Good luck," Keith Waters said as he hung up the phone.

Willy was snoring loudly in the bedroom, and Sister Cordelia was fast asleep on the living room couch when Alvirah tiptoed into the apartment at midnight.

A newspaper was under Cordelia's hands, and her glasses were perched on the end of her nose. Alvirah had removed the glasses and newspaper, unplugged the Christmas tree, and turned out the lights, without disturbing her.

Now, over breakfast, the three of them comfortable in their bathrobes, she related everything that had taken place since she had phoned Cordelia yesterday and asked her to stay with Willy.

"The ransom drop is set for six o'clock tonight, and I intend to be in one of the un-marked cars following Regan," Alvirah declared as she spread a generous lump of butter on her English muffin.

Now that the troublesome dental implant had been mercifully extracted, Willy both sounded and looked more like his old self. "Alvirah, honey, I worry about you being in one of those cars," he began to protest, but then shaking his head, poured himself more coffee. "Useless," he muttered.

Cordelia, the eldest of Willy's six sisters, had entered the convent fifty-three years earlier, at age seventeen. Now the mother superior of a small convent on Manhattan's Upper West Side, she and the four nuns who lived with her spent their time tending to the needy in their parish.

Their many activities included running

an after-school day-care center. Two years earlier, Alvirah had been the one to track down a long-missing child, who turned out to be one of the seven-year-olds in their charge.

After having been her sister-in-law for more than forty years, nothing Alvirah did could surprise Cordelia, and that included winning $40 million in the lottery.

Alvirah and Willy had been most generous with their newfound wealth. As Cordelia put it, "They're the same down-to-earth people they always have been. Willy still comes running whenever any of our people need a plumber. The only difference in Alvirah is, now that she isn't cleaning houses anymore, she's turned into a first-rate amateur detective."

With her regal carriage and no-nonsense air, Cordelia inspired both trust and deference. She also had a way of getting immediately to the heart of the matter.

"Are those ransom drops usually successful?" she asked.

"More successful in fiction than in fact," Alvirah said with a sigh. "And the problem is that if something does go wrong, the kidnappers tend to panic."

Cordelia shook her head. "I'll get every-body praying. I'll just say it's for a special intention."

"We need all the prayers we can get," Alvirah said soberly. "I just feel so help-less."

"Honey, thanks to you they have the kidnapper's voice on tape. That could turn out to be a big help," Willy reminded her.

"Isn't that the truth?" Alvirah exclaimed, clearly cheered. "The detective gave me a copy of the tape last night. Let's listen to it." She got up, retrieved the cassette from her purse and reached into the mahogany cabinet in the living room for her special, highly sensitive tape player, yet another gift from her editor at the *Globe*.

She had spent many hours with her ear cocked to its speaker, listening for nu-ances in the countless conversations she had recorded in her relentless pursuit of justice.

Willy moved the coffeepot out of the way as she set the machine down be-tween the empty bacon plate and the jar of imported raspberry jam.

She snapped in the cassette. "After we hear this, I'm going to get dressed and head over to the hospital. I told Regan I'd come by this morning. What a long day this is going to be for them. There's almost nothing to do now but wait until six o'clock tonight."

"I feel better today, so if there's anything they need for me to do, I'd be glad to help out," Willy offered.

"I'll call you from the hospital," Alvirah promised as she pressed the PLAY button.

The cassette made for grim listening. Willy's frown and the tightening of Cordelia's lips mirrored Alvirah's own sense of anger and concern.

"It's pretty straightforward," Cordelia said when it was over. "It especially breaks my heart to hear that young mother so worried about her boys."

"I'd like to get my hands on that guy," Willy said as he unconsciously punched his left palm with his right fist.

Alvirah was rewinding the tape. "I want to hear it again."

"Did you pick up something, honey?" Willy asked hopefully.

"I'm not sure."

She played it a second time and then again, her eyes tightly closed. Then she turned off the machine. "There's something there that's ringing a bell, but I can't quite figure out what it is."

"Run it through once more," Willy urged.

"No, it won't make a difference right now. It will come to me later. It always does," she said. Frustrated, Alvirah got up from the table. "I can tell it's something important. *But what is it?*"

When Regan and Jack entered the gift shop in the hospital lobby, the carefully made-up fortyish woman behind the counter was yawning. Spotting them, she halfheartedly held up a carefully manicured hand to cover her open mouth.

"Excuse me," she said. "I'm so tired. All this holiday stuff has me aggravated."

"I know what you mean," Regan murmured sympathetically.

"At least you're standing here with a good-looking guy. I haven't had a decent date in months."

"Oh, we're not—" Regan began, but Jack nudged her and smiled at the saleswoman, whose name tag read "Hi. My name is LUCY."

"They told me to get a job in a hospital. You'll meet a lot of doctors. So I get myself hired here to help out for the month of December." She paused briefly as though unable to believe what she was about to report. "Not one doctor has set foot in this place since I started three weeks ago. They all go flying right through the lobby in their white coats."

"Oh dear," Regan found herself murmuring inanely. She cleared her throat. "Well, I'm sorry to bother you but . . ."

"Go ahead," Lucy said in a resigned voice as she picked up her Styrofoam coffee cup. "I'm all ears."

"We need to speak to whomever was working in here last night."

"You're looking at her. Why do you think I'm so tired?"

Regan and Jack exchanged glances. What a stroke of luck was the unspoken mutual thought.

Jack had put the teddy bear with the framed picture in a clear plastic bag he'd gotten from the nurses' station.

Regan held it up. "We think this teddy bear was bought here last evening."

"Bingo."

"You remember selling it?"

"Bingo."

"Can you tell us anything about the person who bought it?"

"Please. Don't get me started. I let him in when I'm closing up, and he takes forever to pick out a teddy bear." Lucy pointed to the display of bears on the shelves. "Do you see any difference between any of them and the one you've got there? I don't.

"Then he reaches down into his shopping bag and pulls out the package that frame was wrapped in. So I stand here—after I've been on my feet all day—and wait for him to unwrap the package, just so he can use the paper again. Then he sticks the frame in the teddy bear's arms and asks me to rewrap the whole thing. So I put it in a box and tied it with a ribbon. Then he takes out his wallet and spends forever getting the exact change out of the secret compartment." She rolled her eyes.

"I can tell you one thing," Lucy concluded, "anyone who goes out with him better know the definition of Dutch treat."

"He paid in cash?" Jack asked.

She looked pained. "Isn't that what I just said?"

"How would you describe him?" Jack continued, a steely edge creeping into his voice.

She paused. "What's this all about anyway? Please don't tell me he's Bill Gates's long-lost brother."

Regan smiled reluctantly. "He left this for my mother, who's a patient upstairs, but he didn't sign the card. She wants to be able to send a thank-you note."

"That's weird," Lucy said, looking genuinely perplexed. "He seemed so pleased with himself, ya know, sticking the frame in the box with the teddy bear and all. I would have thought he'd have signed the card."

"I might be able to figure out who it is if you give me an idea of what he looks like," Regan prodded.

Lucy scrunched up her face. "Not that great," she replied. "You know, around fifty maybe. Brown hair, not much of it, average height, a little wimpy."

"You say he was carrying a shopping bag," Jack said. "Did you happen to notice where it was from?"

She rolled her eyes again. "Oh yeah, I went shopping there once. I bought an outfit that fell apart first time I washed it."

"Where was that?" Regan asked.

"Long's. You heard their commercial? 'I'm longing for Long's.' I'll tell you one thing—I'm not longing for Long's."

"What time do you close here?" Jack asked.

"Usually 7:30. This week we stay open till 9:00. We want to get rid of all this holiday stuff. Once Christmas is over, you can't give it away."

It was obvious that there was nothing more to be learned from her. Regan and Jack crossed the lobby to the reception desk. The obliging clerk there knew who had been on duty the previous evening. "It's my friend Vanessa. Let me phone her."

Regan was dismayed to hear from Vanessa only the same vague description of the man who had left the package. "Did he by any chance mention his name or say that he was a friend of my mother's?"

"He didn't say anything except that he didn't want to disturb her last night."

Regan tried to keep her tone casual as

she said, "I guess whoever left it won't receive a thank-you note."

"A mystery gift for a mystery author," Vanessa said brightly. "Tell her I hope she feels better."

Regan hung up. "She gave the same physical description, but unfortunately didn't add anything, Jack." She turned to the receptionist and thanked her for her help.

As they started to walk away from the desk, Jack pointed to the security cameras that ringed the lobby. In a low tone he said, "I'll get last night's tape. We should be able to pick him out with that big box he was carrying."

"Hello, you two." Alvirah's hearty greeting was unmistakable. Before they could respond, she spotted the object in Regan's hand. With a worried frown, she said, "There's got to be a reason you're carrying that teddy bear in a plastic bag."

"Let's go up to Nora's room," Jack suggested. "It's easier to talk up there."

Five minutes later, when they walked into her room, Nora was hanging up the phone. "I called my broker. The million dollars is being debited from our securities account and credited to Chase Manhattan. From there it will go to the Federal Reserve. I said I was making an overseas investment." She smiled wanly. "Pray God this is the best million dollars we will ever spend."

Jack nodded. "We're doing everything in our power to see that it is."

Together he and Regan told Nora and Alvirah what little they had learned about the donor of the gift. "There was nothing outstanding about him physically. He paid cash. From what we hear, he certainly took his time, so he wasn't nervous. And he was carrying a shopping bag from Long's department store."

"Long's!" Alvirah exclaimed. "Before I won the lottery I used to 'long for Long's.' It's like most of those discount department stores. You have to wade through a ton of junk to find a bargain, but sometimes it happens. Most people see it as a challenge."

She glanced at the frame. "Yup, that looks like a Long's special. Do you want me to check it out for you, Jack?"

Jack knew that Alvirah was a master at ferreting out information. She had an al-

most uncanny way of getting people to
open up. Why not? he thought. Later, if
they could get a halfway decent image
from the security cameras, he would send
one of his squad out to the store to see if
anyone there could ID the guy.

"I think it would be a great idea for Alvirah to go to Long's," Nora said.

For a moment, Regan considered ac-
companying her, then rejected the idea.
The store would most likely be packed
with last-minute shoppers. If the kidnappers called her on her cell phone, she'd
barely be able to hear them.

There was something else. The look on
her mother's face told her that she was
needed here.

"I'll get started looking into the security
tapes," Jack said.

"And I'm off to Long's," Alvirah announced, glad that there was finally some
action she could take.

C.B. and Petey had had a busy morning.
After breakfast, they left the houseboat
and headed west to the isolated and run-
down farm off Route 80 where Petey's

cousin allowed him to keep his outboard motorboat.

As they rattled down the dirt road leading to the farmhouse, C.B. grumbled, "What a dump this place is."

Petey took offense. "It is my cousin's after all. And thanks to him, I've had a place to keep the boat that's going to collect our million dollars, Mr. Hoity-toity. Beggars can't be choosy," he admonished.

"Are you sure your cousin's away?"

"It's Christmastime, remember? Everybody's going somewhere, including us—huh, C.B.? I drove my cousin and his wife to the bus station a few days ago. They should be at my aunt's house in Tampa by now."

C.B. groaned again. "Don't talk to me about relatives."

"Do you miss your uncle?" Petey chuckled, as he jammed on the brake of his paint-stained pickup truck in front of the barn door.

C.B. did not deign to answer. If Uncle Cuthbert had done the right thing, I wouldn't have to put up with this moron, he thought. The closer they got to putting their hands on the money, the more ner-

vous he became that something would go
wrong.

He knew that the location he had chosen for the ransom drop was brilliant. It
was just trusting Petey to get there in one
piece that was the problem. But Petey had
assured him that he could navigate the
waters around Manhattan with his eyes
closed—which C.B. figured was probably
the way he usually did it.

They got out of the car, and Petey ran to
open the barn door. "Ta-daaaah," he cried
as he yanked a cracked and aging tarp
from a decrepit boat, perched atop the
trailer used to haul it to the water.

C.B. almost burst into tears. He hated
his uncle more than ever. "Are you trying
to tell me that thing *floats?*"

By now, Petey had scrambled up the
side of the trailer and jumped into
the boat. "If it had a sail, it could win the
America's Cup," he yelled. He took off
the painter's cap, which was his chapeau
of choice, and waved it at C.B. "Ahoy,
maties!" he cried.

"Get down here, Popeye."

Petey gave him the A-OK sign and
scampered down. "This baby has really

got the juice!" he bragged. "My cousin re-built the motor after I found it in a junk-yard."

"Which is where it belongs. When was the last time that tub was in the water?"

"I went fishing that nice day in October," Petey said, scratching his neck. "Let's see, was it Columbus Day? Or was it the weekend after?"

"I bet it was Halloween," C.B. replied. "Let's hitch that wreck up to the truck and get out of here. It's freezing."

Petey started backing up his vehicle, his head stuck out the window as he urged C.B. to give him some guidance. "How much more room I got there, brother?" he yelled.

C.B. cringed. Before he could answer, Petey had clipped the side of the barn.

After several failed efforts, they finally secured the trailer and went bumping back down the road.

Petey blew his nose and dabbed at his eyes. "I may never see this place again."

"Consider yourself lucky."

C.B. pulled out his notebook, and they went over the plans for the evening. They'd lower the boat into the water in a cove Petey knew about, which was a half-mile south of the houseboat. They'd ditch the trailer there.

At precisely six o'clock, Petey would board the boat and steer it north on the Hudson, through Spuyten Duyvil around the top of Manhattan, to the seawall near the pier at East 127th Street. That was where Regan Reilly would be told to deposit the ransom money. It should take Petey about half an hour to get there.

C.B. would be stationed at the houseboat, and at six o'clock would make the first phone call to Regan Reilly, allowing her to speak briefly to her father and Rosita. He'd tell her to start driving through Central Park. Then he'd hang up before the call could be traced.

He'd rush across the George Washington Bridge and down the East Side Drive calling Regan several more times along the way with instructions as to where she should drive next. "It's known as a delaying action," he explained to Petey. "In case she called the cops, it'll be harder for them to follow her from a distance. For all they know, we have her in sight."

The final instruction would be for Regan

to cross Second Avenue at 127th Street and take the Marginal Street exit and drive onto the isolated dock. There she would be instructed to drop the duffel bag on the seawall and leave.

Once the drop was made, Petey would scramble up, grab the money, hop back on board, and then, with no time to spare, race down to 111th Street, where C.B. would be waiting in the car they had rented under a false name.

Petey would abandon the boat, which, thanks to the fact he never had bothered to register it, and that the motor had been bought in a junkyard, would be untrace-able.

After that, they'd drive back to the houseboat and amuse themselves by counting their money until their flight to Brazil the following night.

"The storm they're forecasting better not screw us up," C.B. said, worried. "The sooner we get out of these parts, the bet-ter."

"*Arriba, arriba!* Cha-cha-cha," Petey sang, tapping his hands rhythmically on the steering wheel.

C.B. decided the best way to cope with

Petey was to ignore him. He pulled one o
Nora Regan Reilly's early books out of his
bag and turned to chapter eight, which
was filled with his own notations.

"I just want to go over this again," he
said, more to himself than to his partner in
crime.

Austin Grady arrived at the office early Fri-
day morning and immediately began re-
viewing the big appointment book on
Luke's desk.

Starting with the present, he studied
Luke's activities day by day, going back
for two months. He found absolutely nothing that brought to mind any mention by
Luke of a difficulty or problem.

The references to the lunches Luke had
had with the late Cuthbert Boniface Goodloe brought an unconscious smile to
Austin's lips and for a moment relieved the
sickening tension that enveloped him. No
bride ever planned her wedding with as
much attention to detail as Goodloe had
dedicated to his funeral, he thought.

Wanting to ensure a full house for his final good-byes, Goodloe had issued spe-

cific instructions. If he died on a weekend, the wake was not to be held until Tuesday. He wanted two full days and nights of viewing, with the funeral to be held on Thursday. That was exactly how it had happened.

"It takes time to notify everyone and get the obituary in the papers," he had said. God knows that plant society got plenty of notice, Austin thought—now we can't get rid of them.

The phone on his desk rang. "This had better not be that Bumbles guy," he muttered to himself. It was Regan. For an instant the sound of her voice gave him a quick hope that maybe she'd say that Luke and Rosita were safe. But, of course, that was not to be.

He told her what he had been doing. "I'm going to keep at it," he promised. "I'm also going to ask some subtle questions around here to see if there's been a problem with any employee that didn't reach our ears."

"Thanks, Austin," Regan said quietly. "Who knows who could have done this. Right now the police are focusing on Rosita's ex-husband. Apparently he has heavy gambling debts, owed to the wrong people."

"That'd motivate you to get your hands on a million dollars any way you can."

"Of course, this could be the work of someone who's been mad at my father for the last ten years." There was a brief hint of levity in Regan's voice. "It's like what they say about us Irish. We forget everything except the grudge."

"Don't I know it, Regan," Austin agreed, thinking of his grandmother, who never forgave her cousin for "stealing her thunder" by scheduling her wedding two weeks before her own long-planned nuptials. Grandma went to her grave sixty years later, still griping about it, Austin thought. The fact that her cousin endured a horrible marriage did nothing to appease her.

"How's your mother doing?" he asked.

"She's hanging in there. I'll be here with her until late this afternoon."

He knew what she meant. "Give her my love, and take care of yourself, Regan."

"Will do," Regan said. "Talk to you later."

Austin had barely replaced the receiver when the phone rang again. He picked it up, the hope always in the back of his mind that it would be Luke's laconic voice saying, as he had at least a thousand times before, "What have we got going on there today, Austin?"

"Austin Grady," he said.

"Ernest Bumbles!" The voice grated through Austin like fingernails on a blackboard.

"Luke is not here," Austin told him firmly. "And no, I don't know when to expect him."

"I'll keep trying," Ernest said cheerfully. "Bye now!"

Luke and Rosita wrapped the thin blankets around themselves as best they could. Even though there was a propane heater, it did little to dispel the bone-chilling dampness of the drafty boat.

"If we get out of here, I'm taking my kids to Puerto Rico for a week," Rosita said. "It'll take me at least that long to warm up."

"*When* we get out of here, I'll send you all, first class," Luke promised.

Rosita smiled wryly. "You'd better watch

your cash flow. Your bank account just
went south a million bucks."

"You owe me half."

"You have some nerve!" This time
Rosita genuinely laughed. "As C.B. keeps
saying, ad nauseam, if you hadn't introduced his dear departed uncle to the
Blossoms, he never would have changed
his will."

"I couldn't get anybody to go to that
dinner," Luke protested. "I had tables to
fill!"

"Do you think Mr. Grady might make the
connection and have the cops check out
our friend C.B.?" Rosita asked.

Luke decided to be honest. "I don't see
why he would. C.B. kept his anger pretty
well hidden at the wake, although I did
catch him stuffing rotting foliage in his
uncle's coffin after viewing hours."

"Are you kidding? Did you tell Mr.
Grady?" she asked hopefully.

"Unfortunately, no," Luke said. "I felt
kind of sorry for C.B. Over the years I've
encountered a lot of understandably emo-
tional people, acting out of character at
the time of a death."

"Then he showed up at the funeral and

the luncheon, and I guess behaved himself. Since you didn't make it to the funeral, they probably realize now that we
were already missing. So no one would tie
him to this," Rosita concluded.

Luke nodded in agreement. "They
wouldn't have any reason to."

"I guess there's no way anyone would
give Petey a second thought either,"
Rosita continued. "You being your usual
unflappable self, Mr. Reilly, never even let
on to him that you were less than thrilled
with the job he did."

"I felt very flappable, but it was easier to
pay him off and send him on his way. And
you must admit, we did get a lot of laughs
out of it."

"We sure did."

"That reminds me, Rosita. If you had
gone out on that date with Petey, we
might not be here."

"I'd rather be here."

Luke chuckled. "I'm forced to agree."

They fell silent for a few minutes; then
Rosita said, "I wonder who's with my
kids?"

"Regan will make sure they're well
looked after."

"Oh, I know that," she said quickly. "It's just that they're probably with someone who doesn't know them, and it always takes a while for Chris and Bobby to feel comfortable with a new baby-sitter." She paused. "I'm sure they're missing me, but they're also probably mad that I haven't come home yet. They've had enough to deal with this past year and a half, with their father deserting them."

"Once you're home, things will be back to normal faster than you think," Luke said, trying to reassure her.

"What bothers me," she said hesitantly, as if she didn't want to vocalize her deepest fear, "is that it's so unbelievable that someone like C.B., who seems so ineffective, would plan and actually pull off a kidnapping. I can't help but wonder what else he's capable of doing, if he decides he doesn't want to leave witnesses."

Luke started to speak, then closed his mouth. There was always the chance the cabin was bugged. He wanted to tell Rosita about his plan to try to communicate to Regan that they were in the vicinity of the subjects of her favorite children's book, the one about the bridge and the ighthouse. He knew it was a stretch, but it was the only card he had to play.

Rosita was absolutely right. C.B. might be capable of a final act of vengeance.

Alvirah hurried past Macy's, heading for Long's department store, around the corner. The traffic had been so heavy she had gotten out of the taxi and jumped into the subway to get downtown. Despite the cold, last-minute holiday shoppers were out in force. Normally she enjoyed window-shopping, but today that was the last thing on her mind.

Alvirah knew that it would be almost impossible to track down the man who had bought the cheap picture frame, but still she was determined to try.

She barreled through the revolving door of Long's and then paused and looked around, getting her bearings. I haven't been here for a while, she thought. Truth to tell, I haven't missed it. But she remembered the layout as though it was yesterday. Men's Department first floor, just like every other store. Retailers know that men hate to shop. When you finally lasso them into the store, the clothes better be popping out at them.

Junk like the frame would definitely be in the basement. There was a line waiting to get on the down escalator. The woman ahead of Alvirah had three small children in tow and looked frazzled.

"Tommy, I warned you not to tell your brothers there's no Santa Claus," she hissed in the eldest child's ear.

"But there isn't!" he protested. "Ma, you don't think that joker in the toy department is really Santa, do you?"

"He's helping Santa out!"

"I heard somebody call him Alvin."

"Never mind," his mother said as she guided her children onto the steps of the escalator.

Precocious, Alvirah thought, amused. But then watching the mother with her children reminded her of the two boys in New Jersey, waiting for their mother to come home.

As they descended into the basement, a banner with the word SALE came into full view. The first floor had been crowded, but down here was a madhouse! Boxes of picked-over Christmas cards were now marked half price. Tables were piled with tree ornaments, Christmas lights, tinsel, and gift wrap. That frame had to come from here, Alvirah decided, when she spotted a counter straight ahead that was covered with a bewildering array of Christmas knickknacks.

Alvirah's bargain-hunting years had left her with the ability to maneuver her body along sales counters without infuriating her fellow shoppers. It worked very well for her today. Within seconds she had found the section where boxes of frames were piled high, an example of each type open and on display. She spotted one that, at a glance, looked just like Nora's.

Excited, she reached around another shopper, lunged for the frame, and whipped out her reading glasses. JINGLE MY BELLS was scrawled across the top in gilt lettering.

"Jingle your own bells," Alvirah muttered, as with a snap of her wrist, she placed the frame facedown on the table. But when she picked up the one next to it, she smiled broadly. I'LL BE HOME FOR CHRISTMAS . . . IF ONLY IN MY DREAMS, it read. This was it!

Alvirah managed to catch the eye of the sales clerk, a good-looking boy who couldn't have been more than eighteen.

"I'll take this," she said, waving the frame at him.

"Let me see which one that is." He reached over and took it from her hands. "Oh, we've got plenty of those." He placed the sample back on the counter and took a box from the only large pile. It was stamped, "Made exclusively for Long's."

Good, Alvirah thought. That answers one question.

"I'm surprised there are any of these left," she said brightly.

He shrugged. "The others went like hotcakes. Not this one."

"Maybe you haven't had them on display long enough," Alvirah said hopefully.

"It seems like they've been there forever." He took her money and rang up the sale.

Alvirah's heart sank. This was like trying to find a needle in a haystack. "Maybe you can help me out," she said hurriedly, knowing the woman at her right elbow was starting to get impatient. "Someone dropped off one of these for my friend in the hospital last night, and the card didn't have a name on it. She feels terrible that she doesn't know who left it. You don't by any chance remember ringing up another one like this, do you?"

"You have to be kidding, lady. You know how busy we've been since Thanksgiving? I won't remember you in two minutes."

"I'll put my picture in one of these frames and send it to you," Alvirah retorted.

"Everything all right here?" a supervisor who appeared from out of the woodwork inquired.

"I was just talking to this nice young man," Alvirah said in a syrupy voice. "He was being so helpful."

"Keep longing for Long's!" the supervisor chirped and rushed off to troubleshoot elsewhere.

"I only fill in on this counter at breaks," the boy said quickly, obviously grateful Alvirah had not complained about him. "The girl who is here most of the time is off today. She'll be back tomorrow morning.

We're opening at nine because it's the last day of Christmas shopping."

"What's her name?"

"Darlene."

"Darlene what?"

"Darlene Krinsky."

"She worked yesterday?"

"All day till closing."

"Thank you," Alvirah said. She'd give this information to Jack Reilly. It was the best she could do for now.

As she walked away, she heard the woman who had been at her elbow say loudly, "Thank God to get rid of Sherlock Holmes."

As the time for the ransom drop approached, the tension in the Major Case Squad at One Police Plaza increased. Everyone who would be involved was in and out of Jack Reilly's office.

It had been a totally frustrating day. The prints they had found in the limo did not belong to anyone on record. The security-camera tapes from the hospital had proven basically useless. The man who had left the gift for Nora Reilly was of average height with slouching posture. When he had entered the hospital, he had been carrying the shopping bag cradled in his arms, virtually hiding his face. Only the back of his head was visible when he entered the gift shop, and when he exited, the huge bow on the box effectively shielded his face from the cameras.

Alvirah had reported on her trip to Long's department store. They had gotten Darlene Krinsky's address and phone number from the store's business office, but so far she hadn't been located. Not surprising, two days before Christmas, Jack thought. She's probably running around shopping, or partying. Not that he expected a talk with her would lead to anything. If that guy hadn't used a credit card for the teddy bear in the gift shop, it was doubtful that he used one for a frame that cost less than ten dollars.

But the conversation with Alvirah did have one direct result. She was going to be riding in the backseat of his car tonight. He still wasn't quite sure how she had talked him into it, but as she pointed out, the only direct link they had to the kidnappers was the tape made because of her quick thinking. It was a fact that could not be denied.

At three o'clock, everyone involved in the ransom drop assembled in Reilly's office. Jack and his close friend, FBI agent Charlie Winslow, jointly ran the meeting.

In painstaking detail, they reviewed every aspect of what would be happening. There would be six cars in the mobile surveillance unit covering Regan Reilly as she followed the kidnappers' instructions. They would stay in touch by portable radios operating on a closed FBI frequency.

The tech unit monitoring Regan's cell phone would immediately convey the instructions through the closed circuit to the mobile unit.

"Our agents have picked up the ransom money from the Federal Reserve," Winslow told them. "Tonight our aircraft will be overhead to track it, wherever it goes."

"You guys," Jack said, nodding to five detectives on the right side of the room, "will be eyeballing the Reillys' apartment building in case the kidnappers try anything as she's leaving the garage. Once she's on the street, you jump in your cars and join the mobile unit. Any comments?"

Dan Rodenburg, a seasoned police veteran of thirty years, shifted in his seat. "I don't like the idea of Regan Reilly driving alone in that car," he said flatly.

Neither do I, Jack thought. "We've thoroughly discussed it with her. She will not further endanger those two lives by having one of us hidden in the car. She was told to keep the police out of it. Regan knows what she's doing; she's a licensed PI of considerable note in California."

Charlie Winslow addressed the look of skepticism on Rodenburg's face. "We've made Regan Reilly an FBI special deputy for this mission. She'll be armed."

Jack continued, "Regan's car will be driven into the garage at her parents' apartment on Central Park South at approximately quarter to six. Regan will be waiting there. The duffel bag with the money will be on the front seat. She'll drive the one block to Sixth Avenue and turn onto the park drive at six o'clock.

Jack paused. "I shouldn't have to say this, but I will. It's just possible that one of you will have the chance to nail whoever makes the pickup. Don't do it. The safety of Luke Reilly and Rosita Gonzalez is what this is all about. Whoever grabs the ransom money may have a prearranged signal that if he isn't back by a certain time, get rid of the hostages. Unfortunately we've seen that happen."

He stood up. "That about wraps it up," he said. "As you know, we have an APB out for Ramon and Junior Gonzalez. Everything points to them."

Just as everyone was getting up to leave, the phone on Jack's desk rang. They all stopped, knowing that he had given orders to hold his calls except any that directly related to the case.

Jack picked up the phone. "Reilly." He listened. "Both of them? . . . Since Tuesday? . . . You checked all the phone records? . . . Big winners, huh?"

He hung up. "The Gonzalez brothers are living it up in Las Vegas, winning back the money they lost in Atlantic City. Which means . . ."

Charlie Winslow finished the thought. "Which means we haven't got any idea who we're dealing with."

• • •

Fred had managed to keep Chris and Bobby busy a good part of the morning by giving them the task of sorting the ornaments and untangling the Christmas lights. While they were absorbed in trying to beat each other at finding the most ornaments that needed new hooks, he quietly went through the apartment. It was a task he found unsettling. It was only the image of Rosita being held against her will that kept him searching for anything that would help bring her home.

It was clear that her life was an open book. The divorce papers showed that the decree had been issued almost a year ago. It granted liberal visitation to the father—something he apparently took little advantage of. The bank statements showed she lived within her means, and there were no dunning letters indicating overdue bills.

Casual questions to the boys about their activities and their mother's friends did not raise any flags.

From everything he could see, Rosita was not romantically involved with anyone and had little or no contact with her ex-husband. This confirmed his initial belief that Luke Reilly must have been the target for the kidnapping, and that Rosita simply had the hard luck to be with him.

At noon he drove with Bobby and Chris to his apartment and got a change of clothes. From there he took them to SportsWorld, an indoor amusement complex, where they had lunch and went on the rides. He kept his cell phone in his breast pocket the entire time. He knew that Keith Waters would call him immediately if there were any developments, or if anyone left a message on Rosita's phone.

They returned to the apartment late in the afternoon. Somehow it seemed to have lost its cozy, welcoming feeling. He could see the way the boys' spirits immediately began to wilt.

Tears began running down Bobby's cheeks. "I thought Mommy would be home by now."

Fred pointed to the Christmas lights and ornaments now in neat piles on the floor. "Come on, we've got to get that tree ready. We want to surprise her when she does get home."

"But we want to save some ornaments for Mommy to put up," Chris reminded him.

"Absolutely. Hey, does Mommy ever play Christmas music?"

"Oh, sure. Mommy loves Christmas music. We have lots of CDs," Chris informed him.

"I choose first." Bobby ran over to the stereo.

As the cheerful sounds of "Rudolph the Red-Nosed Reindeer" filled the room, the phone rang.

Chris raced to grab it, then, disappointment evident in his face, he said, "It's for you, Fred."

It was Keith Waters, calling to tell him that the Gonzalez brothers were no longer suspects. Not a big surprise, Fred thought as he hung up, but still a big disappointment. As the saying went, Better the devil you know. Gonzalez may be desperate for money, but he probably would not have murdered the mother of his children.

Were Rosita and Luke Reilly in the hands of sociopaths?

● ● ●

At 4:30, Nora said to Regan, "You'd better head over to the apartment. Give yourself plenty of time to get there."

Regan could tell how nervous her mother was getting. "I wish you weren't alone," she said.

"I'll keep busy." Nora reached into the drawer of the bedside table and took out her rosary.

"A lap around the beads," Regan smiled.

"A marathon around the beads," Nora corrected her.

Regan bent down and kissed her mother's forehead.

"Be safe, Regan." Nora's voice broke.

Unable to answer, Regan gave her a quick hug, then turned to leave. As she opened the door, she paused and looked back at her mother. "You know, Mom, there's another line that follows 'I'll be home for Christmas . . .' "

" '. . . you can count on me,' " Nora said.

"That's the one."

Regan gave her a thumbs-up and closed the door behind her.

Luke's eyes widened in disbelief when Petey emerged from the bedroom.

Rosita murmured, "Oh my God, I don't believe it."

"Surf's up!" Petey cried. He was moving somewhat awkwardly, weighted down by a full-body wet suit.

"Don't tell me the ransom drop is at a costume party," Luke said.

Rosita nodded. "And he's going as Jacques Cousteau."

"Watch your mouths!" a high-strung C.B. snarled. "There's nothing that says I have to let them know where to find you two."

"That wouldn't be fair," Petey exclaimed, blinking his eyes. He rotated his neck and shoulders. "This thing feels weird. I shoulda gotten it a size smaller."

Always leave room to grow, Luke thought.

"Quit griping and get your goggles and whatever else belongs to that getup," C.B. ordered as he pulled on his own coat and unlocked the door. "It's time to get out of here."

"Hey, wait a minute," Luke said, alarmed that he might not get the chance to talk to Regan. "You told my daughter she could speak to us before she hands over the money. Don't think she'll give it to you if you don't keep your end of the bargain."

"Don't worry," Petey said. "C.B.'s just giving me a ride down to my boat."

"Come on!"

"Okay, okay, don't rush me. I've got a lot on my mind."

They were gone.

But not for long. Ten minutes later, Petey was back. "Forgot the keys to my boat," he said almost apologetically. "Like I told C.B., it's what happens when you rush too much."

At 5:30 Alvirah changed into a comfortable pants suit and rubber-soled shoes for her role as a passenger in Jack Reilly's car, following Regan to the ransom drop. She fastened her sunburst pin on her winter jacket, "That recorder is going to be turned on from the minute I set foot in the car," she announced.

A concerned Willy eyed her sensible shoes. "Honey, if there's a foot chase, you're not going to try to get in it, are you?" he asked anxiously.

"Oh, gosh no, Willy. I couldn't keep up. But if for any reason we get out of the car, I don't want to break my neck. It's getting icy."

"As long as you promise to stay back, no matter what happens."

They went down the hall to the living room where Cordelia was waiting for them.

When Regan had phoned twenty minutes earlier, Cordelia had answered and spoken to her quietly.

"Is your mother alone at the hospital?" she'd asked.

"Yes," Regan had said. "Which bothers me a lot, but she was very adamant about not telling anyone, even her closest friends, about what's going on. She's so afraid of a leak to the media."

"She shouldn't be by herself," Sister Cordelia said firmly. "I'd like to volunteer

to go over there. And I know Willy would
too."

Five minutes later, Regan called back. "
thought my mother wanted to go this
alone, but she says she'd welcome your
company."

They went down in the elevator together.

The doorman hailed a cab for Willy and
Cordelia, then turned to Alvirah.

"A friend is picking me up," she explained.

From the front door, she could see the
garage of the Reillys' apartment building.
At seven minutes of six, Regan drove out
in the dark green BMW. "Godspeed, Regan," Alvirah whispered, as Jack Reilly's
car pulled up to the curb. She ran across
the sidewalk and slid into the backseat.

"Alvirah, this is Detective Joe Azzolino,"
Jack said, indicating the driver. He did not
take his eyes off the BMW as he spoke.

"Nice to meet you, Joe," Alvirah said
crisply. No small talk at a time like this, she
thought.

The long block to Sixth Avenue, as na-
tive New Yorkers still called the Avenue

of the Americas, was clogged with taxis and limousines, picking up and discharging people at the upscale hotels and restaurants that lined Central Park South.

They followed Regan's inch-by-inch progress. "This traffic is perfect for the timing," Jack said with satisfaction. "She won't have to worry about delaying too long at the intersection."

At precisely six o'clock, Regan turned left into Central Park.

A voice came over the FBI closed circuit. "Her cell phone is ringing."

"Have you got it straight?" C.B. asked as he drove down the narrow track that led to the cove where they had secured Petey's boat and hidden the trailer.

"Can a duck swim? Is the Pope Catholic? Do bears—"

"Don't do this to me," C.B. begged. "Let's go through it just once more. You are going to get on that termite-infested piece of wood you call a boat. You are going to watch the time, and at precisely six o'clock turn on the engine and leave."

"Shall we synchronize our watches, me matey?"

C.B. glared at him, then continued. "You will guide that bucket through Spuyter Duyvil, around the north end of Manhattan to the Harlem River—"

"Spuyten Duyvil is Dutch," Petey volunteered. "I think it means 'in spite of the devil.' Current is reeeeeally bad up there. Yup. But no problem for an old salt like me."

"Shut up! Shut up! *Shut up!* I gave you Rosita's cell phone to use—"

"Mr. Reilly's is much newer. You could have given that one to me. But no—"

C.B. braked so violently that Petey was thrown forward. "I could have had a concussion," he said reproachfully.

"To continue, I will call you at about quarter of seven. By then you will be in place, tied to the dock at 127th Street, next to the seawall. I will speak to you briefly. *Try* to understand that the location of a cell phone can be traced in less than a minute."

Petey whistled admiringly. "That's really fast. It's all about technology today, isn't it, C.B.? Me, I like things a little simpler."

"God knows you've proven that," C.B. moaned.

Even with the traffic along River Road, it took C.B. less than ten minutes to drive the half mile from the cove to the houseboat. Every time he made the final turn off the busy thoroughfare, he was acutely aware that a passing police car might trail a car driving down a road that led to a marina closed for the winter.

When they'd hatched the plan, it was Petey who came up with the idea of taking the houseboat he looked after at Lincoln Harbor, a year-round marina in Weehawken, to the isolated pier in Edgewater.

That part of the plan has worked, C.B. grudgingly admitted to himself, as he looked nervously in the rearview mirror. And the next time I turn onto this road, I'll have a million bucks in the backseat.

He made the turn, but drove at a snail's pace until he was sure there was no one behind him. Then he picked up speed for the remaining stretch to the parking area. Once there, he left the car and walked down the dock to the houseboat. The wind was increasing and the temperature dropping. The weather report he had heard on the radio had indicated there was still a chance the storm would blow out to sea.

I don't care where it blows, as long as by then, I've blown out of here with the money, he thought.

The footing was tricky getting on the houseboat. The current was pulling the vessel out, then slapping it back, hard against the dock. Who could possibly want one of these torture chambers? he asked himself as he tried to hoist his out-of-shape body from the pier onto the deck. There was one frightening moment when his legs were pulled into a near-perfect split, one leg on the pier, the other headed out to sea with the boat.

"You'd have to be Gumby to do this as a steady diet," C.B. wailed aloud as he finally got both feet planted on the deck. But this nightmare is almost over, he promised himself as he unlocked the door to the cabin.

Ten minutes later, at precisely 6:00 P.M., he dialed Regan's cell phone. When she answered, in his rehearsed, guttural tone he ordered, "Keep driving north. Your father and Rosita are fine. As a matter of fact, they even listened to your mother on Imus this morning . . . Isn't that right, Luke?" He held the phone up to Luke's mouth.

"I did hear your mother this morning, Regan." Let her get what I'm trying to tell her, Luke prayed. "I can just *see* myself reading your favorite book to you when you were little."

"That's enough!" C.B. said. "Here's Rosita."

"Regan, who's with my boys?"

Before Regan could answer, C.B. pulled the phone back. "Circle the park, Regan. I'll call you back."

He broke the connection. "I'm out of here," he told Luke and Rosita. "Wish me luck."

Her father and Rosita were still alive. The kidnappers were going to collect the ransom. Regan had not realized just how desperately she had feared that something would cause them to panic, and there would be no further word from them.

Circle the park. That was what he had told her to do. There was heavy traffic on the winding park road as far as the Seventy-second Street exit, where a steady stream of cars turned onto Fifth Avenue. Many others veered left to the West Side. Far fewer continued driving north.

Not good, Regan thought. With so little traffic, it will be easier to spot that I'm being followed. Near 110th Street the road curved west, then headed back south. The caller hadn't given her a time limit for the drive through the park, but neither had he said to hurry. He's probably smart enough to know that the cops can fix a location on a cell phone if it's on for more than a minute or so, she thought. That's why he barely let them say anything to me.

Dad heard Mom on Imus this morning, she thought. They had talked about the children's books Mom had sent to Imus for his son. But why did Dad talk about reading to me as a child? He must have *known* he only had a few seconds. And he mentioned my favorite book. Which one *was* it? I can't even remember myself.

She was passing the exit to Ninety-sixth

Street on the West Side. The traffic was picking up.

Last night Mom told me she kept thinking about the days when she and Dad were just starting out. She mentioned their first apartment and selling her first short story. Dad's obviously doing that same kind of reminiscing.

Regan blinked back the tears that started to well in her eyes.

She was passing Tavern on the Green. The restaurant, always brilliantly illuminated, was particularly festive with Christmas lights. When she was little, it had been a special treat to ride the carousel near the Central Park Zoo and then have lunch there.

She was at the southern end of the park, on a strip of road running parallel to Central Park South. She had made almost a complete circle.

The cell phone rang again.

"Sailing, sailing, over the bounty Maine," a goggled Petey sang as he steered his boat north under the George Washington Bridge. But then as the cold, wet air stung his exposed cheeks, he switched to the song he remembered from his first-grade play: "Oh, it's so thrilly when it's chilly in the winter—"

Clunk!

"Iceberg alert!" Petey yelled as the boat bounced up and down. Once again he switched tunes. "... my heart will go onnnnn." He had seen *Titanic* three times. *If I'd been steering that baby, we'd have made it,* he thought.

Petey felt free as a bird. It seemed as if he had the whole river to himself, and he was making great time. He patted the side of the boat. "I'm going to miss you when I'm in Brazil. We've had a lot of fun together. I sure hope the cops find you a good home."

He was almost at the top of Manhattan. "Spuyten Duyvil, here I come," he called as he veered off to enter the narrow tidal strait that connected the Hudson and the Harlem Rivers.

"Feels like I'm in a washing machine," he muttered as the swirling currents fought to twist and turn his aging craft.

"I made it!" he said triumphantly fifteen minutes later, as he tied the boat to the seawall at 127th Street, well hidden under the Triborough Bridge.

Where do all these people think they're going? C.B. fumed as he waited in a line to pay the toll at the George Washington Bridge. They should be home wrapping their presents. Of course, I'll be unwrapping mine in a couple of hours, he mused. The thought cheered him up.

He had written out the instructions he intended to give Regan Reilly. I hope you like to zigzag, he thought, because that's what you'll be doing until seven o'clock.

He checked his watch. It was 6:20. Time to call Regan again, but not until he was out of the vicinity of the bridge. He wanted to be sure to get a clear connection.

As soon as he reached the Harlem River Drive, C.B. pulled out the cell phone. "Time to see the pretty trees on Park Avenue, Regan," he said when she answered.

"What do you think they're up to, Jack?" Joe Azzolino asked his boss as the kidnappers' instruction to Regan to head to Park Avenue was relayed to them from the eavesdropping base at headquarters. "Eagle" was the code name assigned to the operation.

"The obvious answer would be that one of them is tailing her and is trying to spot our cars," Jack said. So why do I have a gut feeling that they've got something up their sleeves that we haven't figured out? he asked himself. They were never going to be able to pinpoint the location of the cell phone. Both calls had been much too brief.

The next call came at 6:35. Regan was told to leave Park Avenue, go up Third Avenue, pull over at 116th Street, and wait.

Jack keyed his transmitter. "Eagle one to all units. Lay back. Give her a little room, but keep her in sight."

Ensconced in the backseat, Alvirah had been remarkably quiet so far, mainly because she had been trying to figure out something that had been bothering her for the last half hour. Finally it came to her, and suddenly she knew why it had struck a chord this morning when she listened to the tape of the kidnappers' first call. One of Nora Regan Reilly's early books had dealt with a kidnapping in Manhattan. In that story, the victim's wife was told to drive up Sixth Avenue from Greenwich Village and enter the park at Central Park South. It's the coincidence of the Central Park South entrance that's been jiggling in my mind, she thought.

When she reached 116th Street, Regan pulled over and double-parked. Azzolino stopped their car at 115th Street and usurped the spot another driver was about to claim. They waited silently.

As more of the plot of Nora's book came back to her, Alvirah realized that in that story, the kidnapper had the wife driving back and forth from the East Side to the West Side. What he really had been doing, however, was maneuvering her farther and farther north, and nearer and nearer to the Harlem River, Alvirah remembered.

In the novel there was something about leaving the ransom money near the river. *Then what?* she wondered. She had read the book so long ago, it was difficult to remember the details. Alvirah frowned in concentration. I've got to put my thinking cap on. But first she thought she should at least say *something* about the similarity of what had happened in Nora Regan Reilly's novel and what was happening now.

"Don't the police have a boat unit on Randall's Island?" she asked.

"Yes, we have a Harbor Unit there," Jack said without turning his head. "Why?"

"Well, it's just that Randall's Island is right next to the Triborough Bridge. It would only take one of your boats a few minutes to travel across the river."

"That's right." There was a hint of impatience in his voice.

"You see, in one of Nora's books that I read a long time ago, the ransom drop was . . ."

At the same moment they heard, "Eagle base to all units. She's been instructed to continue north on Third."

"In Nora's book," Alvirah continued, "the victim's wife drove down a dock or a pier or something and put the money on a seawall. Somebody was waiting in a boat and reached up and grabbed it."

A trailer truck had been racing the light and was now caught in gridlock halfway across Third Avenue. Regan had just cleared the intersection before the truck crossed. Now they were blocked by the truck and could no longer see her. "Eagle one to all units," Jack snapped into the transmitter, "we're locked in. Don't lose her."

"Jack . . ."

"Alvirah, not now, please."

The trailer truck was moving slowly past. Azzolino floored the accelerator. Even running the light, they were now a full block behind Regan.

They were passing 123rd Street.

Somehow Alvirah was absolutely sure of what would happen next. Dollars to donuts, Regan would be instructed to drive on a lonely road along a dock on the Harlem River. They'll tell her to leave the money on a seawall.

"Jack, I know you'll think I'm crazy, but you've got to listen to me," she said. "Those kidnappers have read Nora's books, and they're following one of her plots. You've got to get some of your men over to the river around the Triborough

Bridge right away. There's a boat there waiting to make the pickup."

We need this, Joe Azzolino thought.

"Eagle base to all units. She's been told to take a right on 127th Street."

Marginal Street, Alvirah thought. That's the road she'll be told to take.

"Jack, listen to me. You've got to get a boat on the river or you'll lose them."

"Alvirah, for God's sake—"

"Eagle base to all units. She's been told to drive east and take the exit . . ."

". . . to Marginal Street," Alvirah finished with him.

Marginal Street appeared to be not so much a road as a long, bumpy, desolate dock. Regan drove along it slowly, not sure how far to go.

The phone rang again. "Drive as far as the Triborough Bridge and stop." Again the connection was broken.

Wild with tension, C.B. phoned Petey. "She'll be there in thirty seconds!"

Petey squealed with delight, then lowered his voice until it seemed to be coming from somewhere deep in his toes.

"Ready, partner." He was proud of himself that, even in this moment of great stress, he remembered to disguise his voice.

Regan's eyes darted from one side to the other, but she saw no sign of anyone nearby. She reached the underspan of the bridge and stopped. Overhead she knew hundreds of cars were passing to and from the three boroughs, but this place felt so removed from all that activity that it might have been on another planet.

She looked to either side of her car, then in the rearview mirror. This road was so isolated that the appearance of any other vehicle would make it apparent to the kidnappers that she was being followed. *Don't come too close, Jack,* she thought, *you'll scare them off. I can handle myself.*

The cell phone rang and she grabbed it. "I'm here," she said.

"Get out of the car. Take the duffel bag to the seawall and put it down on the edge. Return to your car. Back up slowly. When all the money is safely in our hands, you will learn the whereabouts of your father and Rosita. If it is not . . ."

The phone went dead.

Regan got out of the car, walked around it, and opened the passenger door. Jack had told her the duffel bag weighed twenty-two pounds. She grabbed it by the handle, lifted it in her arms, and carried it to the seawall. As she leaned over to lay it down, she realized that there was a boat tied to the wall only a few feet away.

A boat, she thought with dismay. They're making the pickup in a boat! The mobile unit from the Major Case Squad would be useless.

But the duffel bag was bugged, and the overhead aircraft would follow it to its destination. Pray God that that was where they were keeping Dad and Rosita.

Wanting desperately to see anything that might later help her identify the kidnappers, Regan allowed herself a fleeting sideward glance toward the boat as she straightened up. The only thing she could discern was that whoever was on the vessel was wearing a wet suit.

Before she could get back in the car, she heard a voice from the boat call out, "Thank you very much, Regan."

. . .

"Eagle one to all units. Stay back. Pickup is probably by boat."

They could see Regan's car roll to a halt nearly two blocks down the dock.

"She's been told to get out of the car and leave the money on the seawall," Eagle base reported.

"Hook me up to the Harbor Unit," Jack snapped.

Alvirah listened as in terse, urgent phrases, Jack told the commander there what he needed. "Follow the boat they're in . . . no running lights . . . do not apprehend . . ."

"Jack, Regan is backing up. She must have made the drop." Azzolino pointed to the BMW, which was slowly coming toward them.

Jack jumped out and was opening Regan's door before the wheels stopped rolling. "They were on a boat." It was not a question.

"There appeared to be just one of them. He was wearing a wet suit," Regan said, shaking her head. "I couldn't believe it. That weirdo called out to me by name to say thank you. It was chilling. He sounded almost like a little kid."

"He's a little kid who is very familiar with your mother's books," Jack said grimly. He looked out at the water. A Harbor Unit boat, its running lights off, could be seen heading down the river.

By now that guy's probably a mile away and ditching the boat, Jack thought. Our only hope now is the tracer in the duffel bag.

I should have listened to Alvirah.

Petey the Painter had never experienced such excitement. His head was pounding, his brain was throbbing, his ears were ringing, his hands were trembling. He had never been so deliriously happy in his life.

There was a million dollars at his feet! A million dollars for him and C.B. to have a good time with. He wished they were going to Brazil tonight. He really deserved a vacation. The Copacabana, he thought. Beautiful girls! He heard that a lot of them went topless on the beaches down there. Woo-woo!

Inside his gloves his fingers were freezing. They'd warm up when he was counting the money.

The river's current was going north. But bucking against it didn't slow him down. The pier at 111th Street was right ahead. And so was the pedestrian bridge he would use to cross over the FDR Drive.

C.B. would be waiting there for him in the car. He would jump in with the money, and off they'd go.

He pulled up to the pier and quickly tied the boat to it. Now for the tricky part, he thought. He stood up, his feet parted, and braced himself to pick up the bag and hoist it to the pier. He reached down and cradled the bag lovingly in his arms. No mother had ever held her newborn with more tenderness.

It was time to go. Whenever God closes a door he opens a window, Petey thought sadly as he looked at his boat for the last time. Overwhelmed, he bent over to kiss the bow. As his lips touched the briny surface, a wind-whipped wave slapped against the boat. Petey felt himself toppling forward.

SPLASH!

As Petey belly-flopped into the water,

his precious cargo went flying out of his hands, landing a few feet beyond his reach. The swirling current of the East River now claimed it as its own and began to whisk it northward.

Desperately, Petey began a furious dog-paddle in an effort to retrieve it but within seconds realized it was hopeless. The current was trying to suck him under. He managed to get back to the boat, which he no longer felt like kissing, and grabbed onto the side for dear life.

What can I do? What can I do?! he thought, his mind a jumble of confusion.

There was only one thing he could do, he thought, gasping for breath. Drag himself up to the pier, cross the pedestrian bridge, and meet C.B. He'll get over it, he kept telling himself. After all, it's only money, and I could have drowned.

Five minutes later, a soggy Petey was tapping on the window of C.B.'s rental car. "I've got good news and bad news," he began.

"You've done everything you can," Alvirah assured Regan as they drove from Marginal Street to the hospital. "And you said the guy in the boat sounded polite and even thanked you. That's a good sign."

"I hope so. Alvirah, I just can't believe these people got the idea for the location of the ransom drop from one of my mother's books. I read that book so long ago, I'd forgotten all about it."

"You'd have been just a kid when it came out."

Regan sighed. "My mother has written so many books, even she forgets the details of plots from twenty years ago. I'm trying to think how that one ended."

Alvirah knew. The kidnap victim had never been heard from again.

They exited the FDR Drive at Seventy-first Street and parked the car on First Avenue. Entering the hospital, they passed the gift shop on the way to the elevator. Inside they could see that Lucy was on duty. She and Regan exchanged glances, and Lucy waved.

"Still here," Lucy called out.

"She's the one you talked to this morning about the teddy bear, isn't she?" Alvirah asked.

"Yes."

In the elevator up to Nora's room, Alvirah made a mental note to drop in on Lucy on the way out. Sometimes you don't know how much you know, she told herself. Maybe if I talk to her, I can jiggle that girl's brain a bit. It's worth trying.

Regan opened the door of the room. Nora, Sister Cordelia, and Willy greeted her and Alvirah with expressions of stunned disbelief.

"What?" Regan asked through suddenly dry lips. "Did you hear something about Dad?"

"Jack just called here," Nora said. "He didn't want to tie up your cell phone. He thinks there's a good chance you'll be getting another call very soon."

"About finding Dad and Rosita?" Regan asked, somehow knowing the answer.

"No." Nora paused. "The Harbor Police just plucked the duffel bag with the million dollars out of the East River."

"Oh my God," Regan gasped.

Nora's face was ashen. "Jack thinks it means one of two things. Either they dropped it by mistake—which would be good—or for some reason they panicked because they suspected there was a tracking device in it." Her voice rose sharply. "Regan, if we get a second chance with these people, there's going to be nothing but money in the bag."

"Mom, the only reason for using the tracking device was in the hope that they would take the money to where they're keeping Dad and Rosita. You know that."

They all knew that, but Regan could see the same fear on all the faces around her that she was sure was on her own. Whether it was a bungled ransom drop or a deliberate discarding of the money, it meant that her father and Rosita were in the hands of some very unhappy abductors.

"You were kissing your boat good-bye?!" C.B. howled as he drove up First Avenue. "You couldn't do it while you were waiting for Regan Reilly? You could have smothered it with kisses!"

"Would you turn up the heater? I think I caught a chill in that river." Petey sneezed. "See?"

C.B. punched the steering wheel. "You

had the million dollars in your hands and you let it go."

"No use crying over spilled milk," Petey said. "I could have drowned, you know. Did you ever think about that?"

"Did you ever think about the fact we have no money, we have two hostages on our hands, and . . ."

"We should have set up a petty-cash fund for their food. I had to fork over six bucks for . . ."

"Petty-cash fund! You just lost us a million dollars!" C.B.'s throat was starting to hurt from the strain of shouting.

"We'll figure a way to get it back," Petey said optimistically.

"Just what do you suggest?" C.B. asked, his voice dropping to a dangerously low level.

"Good question."

"Do you think maybe we should call Regan Reilly and tell her what a bumbling idiot you are?"

"Uh-uh."

"Do you think we should get on that plane to Brazil with barely enough money for a week's vacation?"

"Uh-uh."

"Do you think we should release Reilly and Rosita, and then have a beer with them at Elsie's?"

"Uh-uh."

"Then what do you suggest?"

"It's hard to think when I'm cold." Petey leaned back and reached for the trash bag on the backseat. "Being that we don't need this anymore, I'm going to use it to try and get warm." He started ripping it at the seams.

"I had thought of everything," C.B. moaned. "I knew that they'd be able to come up with the million bucks. I knew that they'd probably call the cops. I knew that there'd almost certainly be a tracking device attached somewhere to the bag. I read a lot of mysteries, you know."

"Reading is important," Petey said approvingly.

"... I would have dumped the money from the duffel bag into that trash bag, which I would now like to wrap around your neck. And that duffel bag should now be lying in the middle of 111th Street instead of floating around the East River."

Petey shifted in his seat, the trash bag

crinkling around him. "Wait a minute. You think they called the cops?"

"Of course. They always call the cops."

"That irritates me. We asked her not to, right?" Petey complained. "You should let her know that when you talk to her."

C.B. gave him a withering look, but then his eyes narrowed. The best defense is a good offense, he thought, as an idea began to form in his mind.

Shortly after 8:30, Jack Reilly joined Regan, Alvirah, Willy, and Cordelia in Nora's hospital room.

"I understand that I was a big help to my husband's kidnappers," Nora said.

"Apparently you were," Jack agreed. "I've got a little more information," he told them, "but not as much as I'd like. A boat was found tied to the pier at 111th Street. We're pretty sure it was abandoned by the kidnappers. It's on its way to the lab now. That was also probably the place where the bag with the money went into the water."

"How would you know that?" Sister Cordelia asked.

"It was at that point that the guys on the aircraft tracking the bag of money realized it had switched directions and started heading north."

"Did the boat have any markings?" Regan asked.

"None. And it's obviously a rebuilt motor, which means it probably can't be traced. We're hoping for fingerprints."

There was a moment of silence. Everyone understood that the next move was up to the kidnappers.

Sister Cordelia squeezed Nora's hand. "It's time we let you get some rest. We'll keep praying."

"I'm glad you were here," Nora said sincerely. She looked at Willy. "I can't believe you made me laugh."

He smiled at her. "I'm saving my best stories for when you feel better."

Alvirah turned to Regan. "Now keep me posted. Call at any hour. I'm going to do some homework with those tapes."

Jack had given her a cassette with all the calls from the kidnappers Eagle base had taped. "This might not be orthodox, but after what happened today, I don't care," he had said. "Alvirah, next time you try to tell me something, I swear I'll listen."

The doctor came in as Alvirah, Willy, and Cordelia were leaving. He obviously knew there was a personal problem of some kind but did not probe. "How's that leg feeling?" he asked.

"Not the best," Nora admitted, the weariness in her eyes clearly visible. Reluctantly she agreed to take a painkiller.

Regan was sure that if her mother were left alone, she'd fall asleep. "Mom, I'm going to run downstairs and get a cup of coffee. I won't be long. Can I bring you back anything?"

"No, but you should eat something."

Jack walked out with Regan. "Okay if I join you for that coffee?"

Once in the cafeteria, Jack prevailed on Regan to have a sandwich.

"We're certainly keeping you from enjoying the holidays," Regan said. "I can't believe tomorrow is Christmas Eve. You must have had plans."

"My family will still be there when I get home. My parents live in Bedford, and that's where the whole clan will be this week. There are so many of us, they won't even notice I haven't shown up yet."

Regan smiled. "Being an only child, if I don't show up it's noticeable."

Jack laughed. "If you were one of ten, it would be noticeable."

That remark would have snapped my mother awake, Regan thought, smiling. Kind of wakes me up too.

They talked about what the kidnappers might do next.

"My biggest fear is that absolutely nothing will happen next," Regan admitted.

"Regan, keep in mind that you talked to your father and Rosita less than three hours ago," Jack said.

"Those few words my father said keep running through my mind. He mentioned reading my favorite book to me when I was a little girl. I thought at the time he was just being nostalgic, like last night when my mother was reminiscing about when they were newlyweds." She shook her head. "But now I'm not so sure. I have a feeling he was trying to tell me something."

"What was your favorite book?" Jack asked.

"For the life of me, I can't remember."

Restlessly Regan tapped her hands on the table. "Maybe my father brought it up because my mother and Imus talked about children's books this morning."

"More than likely that's all it was. But you know as well as I do that kidnap victims often try to pass messages if they possibly can."

"Oh, it's you two again!" The call came from across the room.

They looked up to see Lucy from the gift shop bearing down on them.

"Can't get enough of each other, huh?" Her eyes darted around. "I always take a walk through here before I go home. As usual, no Dr. Kildares in sight." She shrugged. "What are you going to do? Say, your mother must be some stickler for writing thank-you notes. One of her friends was just in the shop, asking about the guy who bought the teddy bear."

Regan and Jack looked at each other. "Alvirah," they said in unison.

Willy and Cordelia were waiting for Alvirah on a couch in the lobby when she emerged from the gift shop.

"Well, I did find something out," she reported.

"What did you learn, honey?" Willy asked.

"The man who sent that teddy bear with Luke Reilly's picture was carrying a Long's shopping bag."

"You knew that."

"Yes, but Lucy—that's the clerk's name—remembered something else. There was a red jacket or sweater, or at least some sort of red clothing, in the bag."

"So?" Cordelia asked.

"Oh, I know it's not much, but it's something," Alvirah said, sighing. "Maybe it will help jog the memory of the salesclerk at Long's when I talk to her tomorrow."

Cordelia was going home.

Alvirah and Willy put her in a cab, then hailed one for themselves. "Two-eleven Central Park South," Willy said.

Even though it was late and the temperature was steadily dropping, the streets were filled with people. When the cab reached the area of the Plaza Hotel, Alvirah remarked wistfully, "It always looks so festive around here during the holidays.

' 'Tis the season to be jolly,' and all that."
She shook her head as she remembered
the sadness in Nora's eyes.

When they got home, she changed into
her favorite old robe, made a pot of tea,
and settled at the dining room table. I began the day with this and I'll finish the day
with this, she thought as she turned on her
recorder.

She listened to all the tapes, playing
them in the order they had been recorded.
First, the original call from the kidnappers,
then the conversation with Fred Torres at
Rosita's home. She replayed that tape
twice, each time stopping at one point.
"Probably doesn't mean a thing, but it's
worth asking him about," she said aloud
as she jotted a phrase on her memo pad.

Willy joined her as she was playing the
tapes of the kidnapper giving directions to
Regan.

"What impression are you getting of that
guy?" Alivrah asked.

"He's disguising his voice," Willy said.
"He's smart enough to get off the phone
fast, so his location can't be traced. He
planned that ransom drop mighty carefully."

"He was smart enough to realize the plot Nora used could work for him, and it did to a point. Now listen to this one." She played the tape of the call in which Luke and Rosita spoke to Regan as she started driving into Central Park.

"Hear anything special?" she asked Willy.

"It's not as clear as the calls that came after it."

"That's right. The reception isn't as good. That's probably because of the location where they're being kept. You know, there can be a lot of interference in some areas." Alvirah played the tape again. "Did you notice anything about what Luke Reilly said?"

"Well, the poor guy's obviously reminiscing about his life. I did that when I was kidnapped. And . . ."

"And what?"

"He kind of puts a big emphasis on the word 'see.' It's almost like he's trying to tell her something."

"That's exactly what I was thinking."

Willy glanced at the pad. "What's that mean?" He pointed to a notation she had made.

"It's something I want to run by Fred
Torres tomorrow. Rosita told him that Luke
Reilly always 'kept his cool.' I want to find
out if Rosita talked about any specific situation where he had to 'keep his cool.' "
She looked at her watch. "It's eleven
o'clock, and still no word from Regan.
That means she hasn't heard from the kidnappers."

"Maybe they're trying to figure out their
next move," Willy suggested.

"Then they better figure it out soon.
What worries me is that the longer Luke
Reilly is missing, the more likely that word
of his kidnapping will get out. If it ends up
in the headlines, God knows what will
happen."

C.B. did not attempt to hide the situation
from Luke and Rosita. When he and Petey
arrived back at the houseboat, he told
them exactly what had happened.

"You can't make this stuff up," Rosita
said, glaring at Petey as he went into the
bedroom to change out of his wet suit.

"You actually used a scenario from my

wife's book for the ransom drop?" Luke asked incredulously.

"It almost worked," Petey called from the bedroom. "Has she got any other kidnapping stories we could take a look at?" He poked his head out the door. "We can't miss our flight tomorrow night. The planes are overbooked."

"I've read all her novels," C.B. said shortly. "She doesn't have any other kidnappings."

Oh yes she does, Luke thought. The other one had come to mind only a few weeks ago when he had business in Queens and took the wrong turn coming out of the Queens-Midtown Tunnel. He had found himself on the same route she'd used for a ransom drop in one of her early short stories. He remembered it because Nora had been pregnant with Regan when she wrote that story, and since she had been ordered to stay in bed, he had driven around and checked out the route she was planning for the kidnappers to use.

"What do you intend to do now?" he asked C.B.

"At some point I'm going to call your

daughter and tell her she'd better be able to come up with another million dollars. Unless, of course, the cops have already recovered our money from the East River.'

There was a note of desperation in his voice. They have to get out tomorrow night, Luke thought, and they can't go without the money. "When you put me on the phone again, I'll tell my daughter to be sure to get it for you."

"You bet you will. But first I've got to figure out a new place for her to leave it," C.B. blustered.

It's worth a shot, Luke thought. By now, Nora must have realized that they had used a ransom-drop location that was in one of her books. This time, would she think about that short story and talk to the cops about it?

It was probably crazy. A one-in-a-million shot, if not totally hopeless. But like his earlier effort to convey to Regan that they were in the vicinity of the GW Bridge and the lighthouse, it at least made him feel as if he was doing something to try and save their lives.

"You know, C.B.," he began, his tone friendly, "a couple of weeks ago I had to pick up the remains of a client's grand-mother from a small nursing home in Queens. When I came through the Midtown Tunnel and exited on Borden Avenue on the Queens side, I got lost. In only a few blocks, I found myself in a totally deserted area right underneath the Long Island Expressway. If I were planning a kidnapping, I think I'd use that area for a ransom drop. Check it out yourself and you'll see what I mean."

C.B.'s eyes narrowed. "Why are you be-ing so helpful?"

"Because I want to get out of here. The sooner you have the money, the sooner you'll make the call telling them where to find us."

"I feel better," Petey announced as he emerged from the bedroom in a sweat suit. "Nothing like a dry change of clothes." He pulled a Mountain Dew out of the tiny refrigerator. "I heard what you were saying, Mr. Reilly. You're really using the old noodle. I know exactly where you're talking about. I got lost there, too, on my way to a job. I wasn't going to pick up a stiff though." He turned to C.B. "It's perfect. We'd be nice and near the airport. They get mad if you don't check in at least two hours before flight time. Sometimes they give your seat away. It happened to my cousin—"

"Petey!" C.B. shrieked.

"Oh, leave him alone," Rosita said. "I'd love to hear the rest of the story."

Luke could tell that C.B. was mulling the suggestion of the drop site over in his mind.

C.B. reached into his pocket and pulled out a folded sheet of paper. On it he had printed the step-by-step directions he had given Regan earlier. He turned the paper over. "Okay, Mr. Reilly, fire away. Petey and I are going to take a drive tonight and see if you're as smart as your wife."

"Go back out in that cold?" Petey protested.

Luke gave C.B. the directions, then said, "Before you go, you'd better call my daughter and let her start arranging to get the money. And give her a break. She's got to be worried."

"Let her worry."

It was nearly midnight before C.B. and Petey returned to the houseboat. Rosita had dozed off, but Luke was wide awake. Over and over in his mind, he had been revising the few words he would be allowed to say to Regan when the next call was made.

When C.B. turned on the light, Rosita opened her eyes and sat up.

"Well?" Luke asked him.

"Not bad," C.B. said. "It might do."

"Scary around there!" Petey exclaimed. "I told C.B. to lock the car doors."

"I think your daughter should be plenty worried by now," C.B. said. "Do you think it's too late to call?"

"Somehow I doubt it," Luke said.

Regan was sitting by a sleeping Nora when the cell phone rang. Please let it be them, she prayed, her heart pounding. She picked it up. "Hello," she said quietly.

"Did you recover the money?"

Regan stiffened. "What do you mean?"

"I mean," C.B. said angrily, "we could tell there was a tracer in the duffel bag. Don't do that again. Have another million ready, or you'll regret it. I'll call you at four o'clock tomorrow afternoon. Here's Daddy."

"Regan, at this point, I'm seeing *red*. Do as he says and get us out of here."

The line went dead.

Saturday, December 24th

Fred had heard from Regan shortly after midnight. She'd told him about the kidnappers' call, and how they had warned her not to have a tracking device in the next ransom delivery. She hadn't spoken to Rosita, but her father had said, "Get *us* out of here."

After the call, Fred had tossed and turned on the couch. If the next drop doesn't work, they'll give up, he thought. And they won't leave witnesses.

At 3:00 A.M., he had taken the blanket and pillow and stretched out on top of Rosita's bed. Before long, he was joined by two troubled little boys who curled up against him and fell back asleep.

"Mommy's sick, isn't she?" Bobby had asked quietly when they woke up.

"Maybe she got sick like Grandma did,

and went to Puerto Rico without us," Chris suggested.

"All your mommy cares about is getting home and being with you guys," Fred said reassuringly. "But Mrs. Reilly really needs her now."

"She won't stay with Mrs. Reilly tomorrow, will she?" Bobby asked.

Tomorrow, Fred thought. Christmas Day. What could he possibly tell them if she wasn't back then? And what was he going to tell Rosita's mother when she phoned to wish them a merry Christmas, as she almost certainly would.

To help pass the time, he took the boys out to breakfast, but they turned down his offer of another trip to SportsWorld.

"We should be there in case Mommy gets home," Chris said solemnly.

Ernest Bumbles woke up on Christmas Eve in what was for him a very grumpy mood. He still hadn't been able to catch up with Luke Reilly, even though he had stopped by Reilly's Funeral Home twice yesterday—once in the afternoon and again in the evening.

"A gift deferred is a gift denied," he told Dolly as he packed his suitcase for their annual trip to his mother-in-law's.

Dolly knew all about Ernest's passionate nature. When he felt something, he felt it with all his heart. When he wanted something, he let nothing stand in his way. That's why, year after year, he had been unanimously reelected president of the Seed-Plant-Bloom-and-Blossom Society. But he was also a caring man. It was no wonder he never had a plant die on him.

"Bumby," Dolly said gently. "We're not leaving until late this afternoon. Why don't we drive by Mr. Reilly's house and ring the bell on our way out of town?"

"I don't want to seem like a pest."

"Oh, hush. You never could."

Nora had awakened to hear Regan talking to Luke's abductor. When the brief conversation was abruptly terminated, Regan told her, word for word, exactly what had been said.

The bedside phone rang almost immediately.

"They can't know there was a tracer in

that bag," Jack said firmly. "They're bluff-ing. I wouldn't be surprised if the guy on the boat accidentally dropped it into the water."

"I wouldn't be surprised by that either," Regan said, "but my mother is adamant that there be no tracer in the bag this time."

"I understand," Jack said. "Regan, re-mind your mother that it's a good sign you talked to your father again. When he spoke to you, he said, 'I'm seeing red.' Is that an expression he uses when he's an-gry?"

"I've never heard him say that in my life," Regan said. "Neither has my mother."

"Then he's definitely trying to tell you something," Jack said. "See if you or your mother can make the connection."

Regan and Jack agreed to talk in the morning, then Regan had phoned Alvirah and Fred.

It was another near-sleepless night for her and Nora as they tried to make sense of what Luke had said and to remember what Regan's favorite book had been as a child.

Nora said, "Regan, when your father came home from work, you always ran to him with a book in your hand. I just can't remember what your favorite one would have been. Could it have been one of the fairy tales? 'Snow White,' or 'Sleeping Beauty,' or maybe 'Rumplestiltskin'?"

"No," Regan said. "It wasn't any one of them."

Around dawn, they both dropped off into a light, uneasy sleep.

Neither one of them had wanted breakfast. Then at eight o'clock, Nora was taken for X rays. When she returned to the room at 9:00, Regan went down to the cafeteria and brought back containers of hot coffee.

"Regan, while I was waiting to be x-rayed, something came to me that I think is important," Nora said after she took the first sip.

Regan waited.

"It is absolutely weird that a scenario from one of my early books was used for the ransom drop yesterday. That card with your father's picture was signed 'Your number-one fan.' If that person is the kidnapper, it's possible he's familiar with all my work."

"That's very possible," Regan agreed. "In which case we're dealing with an obsession. But what are you saying?"

"As I lay there, it came to me that I wrote another kidnapping story, a long time ago."

"You did? I never read it."

"I wrote it when I was pregnant with you," Nora recalled. "It was a short story, not a book, but it described in detail a ransom drop in Queens." She bit her lip. "My doctor had ordered bed rest when I was working on it, and I remember that Dad came up with the suggestion for the location of the drop. He drove out there, took pictures, and drew a map, even to the point of marking the best place to leave the suitcase of money. I was paid all of one hundred dollars for the story when it was published, and Dad joked that I should give him half."

Regan smiled briefly. "That sounds like Dad." Despite the stab of pain that hit her heart, she felt a surge of hope. "Mom, suppose you're right and the kidnapper *is* a pathological fan who's acting out your plots. It's very possible he's somehow gotten his hands on that story and will use that plot for the drop tomorrow. If we knew ahead of time the kind of directions he's likely to give me, the police can stake out the route beforehand without being visible. Where in Queens was the ransom drop?"

"God, Regan, it was so long ago, and as I said, Dad researched it for me. All I remember is that it was near the Midtown Tunnel."

"You must have a copy of the story."

"It's home somewhere in the attic."

"What about the magazine it was in?"

"It bit the dust a long time ago."

There was a tap at the door. The doctor breezed into the room, a holiday smile on his face, a batch of X rays under his arm. "Morning, ladies," he said. "How's my favorite patient?"

"Pretty good," Nora said.

"Good enough to go home?"

Nora looked at him, surprised. "You were pretty insistent on my staying for at least three days."

"You had a nasty fracture, but the swelling is going down nicely. The X rays look okay. You must be anxious to get out of here. Just be sure to keep that leg elevated." He turned to Regan. "Maybe next year, you and your parents will make it to Maui for Christmas."

"I hope so," Regan said. More than you can imagine, she thought.

When he left the room, Nora and Regan looked at each other.

"Regan," Nora said, "run and get the car. I'll get checked out of here. There are an awful lot of boxes in that attic."

At five of nine, Alvirah was in the forefront of the throng of last-minute shoppers waiting for Long's department store to open its doors. Unlike the others, she did not have a list of gifts to buy, most of which would probably be returned forty-eight hours later. She had already phoned Fred to ask about why Rosita had told him Luke "always kept his cool." He assured her that Rosita was only referring to humorous situations.

At 9:01, she was on the down escalator, headed for the basement. Fast as she was, there were already shoppers at the counter where the Christmas knickknacks had been further reduced to almost give-away prices. They must have slept in the aisles last night, she thought, as with mounting impatience she waited to get the only salesgirl's attention.

The customer ahead of her, a thin, white-haired septuagenarian, was cross-ing names off her shopping list as she handed one picture frame after another to the clerk. "Let's see. That takes care of Aggie and Margie and Kitty and May. Should I get one for Lillian? . . . Nah, she didn't give me anything last year." She picked up one of the "Jingle My Bells" frames. "Disgraceful," she proclaimed. "That'll be all."

"Are you Darlene Krinsky?" Alvirah asked the young saleswoman when she fi-nally got her attention.

"Yes." Her voice was wary.

Alvirah knew she had to make it fast. She took out the frame she had pur-chased the day before. "My friend is in the hospital." That might get her sympathy, she thought. "Someone left one of these frames for her on Thursday night and didn't sign his name. We think he may have bought it when he was on the way to the hospital, because we know he was carrying a Long's shopping bag with some red clothing in it. He's a man of medium height, with thinning brown hair, and about fifty years old."

Krinsky shook her head. "I wish I could help you." With her eyes she indicated a group of teenagers who were waving the knickknacks they had selected, anxious to get her attention. "You can see how crazy it is around here."

"He was carrying an old wallet and may have counted the change out very carefully," Alvirah persisted.

"I'm sorry, I'd really like to help, but . . ." She trailed off. "I hope your friend feels better." She took a Santa Claus music box out of the hands of one of the teenagers.

It's hopeless, Alvirah thought dejectedly as she turned away from the counter.

"Wait a minute," the clerk said softly to herself as she started to ring up the music box.

As Alvirah reached the escalator, she felt a tap on her shoulder. "The clerk at that counter is calling you," a young man said.

Alvirah rushed back.

"You say he had a bag with red clothing in it? I know who it might be. One of the guys who plays Santa Claus was down here the other night. I'm sure that was the frame he bought. He tried to get an employee discount."

That's got to be him, Alvirah thought. "Can you tell me his name?"

"No. But he might even be upstairs now. The toy department is on the third floor."

"You must be talking about Alvin Luck," the manager of the toy department, a pinched-faced man in his late fifties, said to Alvirah. "He was working here Thursday evening, and no doubt was carrying his uniform home to press. We insist that our Santas set a good example for the children."

"Is he due in soon?"

"He doesn't work here anymore."

"He doesn't?" Alvirah asked, dismayed.

"No. He turned in his uniform yesterday. When we hired him, he made it very clear he couldn't work on Christmas Eve."

"Was he here last night?"

"No. He left at four o'clock."

"Would you have his address or phone number?"

The manager looked sternly at Alvirah. "Madam, we have total respect for our employees' privacy. That information is strictly confidential."

Jack can get it in a minute, Alvirah thought, as she thanked the man and rushed to a telephone. And anyhow, he'll take over from here. If Alvin Luck *is* involved in the kidnapping, Jack will find out fast.

Alvin Luck and his mother handed their tickets to the usher at the door of Radio City Music Hall. Since he was a child, it had been their tradition to take in the Christmas Spectacular on Christmas Eve, and then treat themselves to a special lunch. In the old days they had dined at Schrafft's, and they both agreed that things weren't the same since that venerable purveyor of chicken à la king had closed its doors.

After lunch, weather permitting, they would take in the sights of Fifth Avenue.

Today they thoroughly enjoyed the show, lingered over lunch, and then prevailed on a security guard to take their annual picture in front of the tree in Rockefeller Center. All the while they were blissfully unaware that half the police department in New York City was on the lookout for them.

It was nearly 11:30 when Regan, with Nora sitting sideways in the backseat of the car, her injured leg across the seat, pulled into their driveway in Summit, New Jersey. Alvirah and Willy were in a car right behind them.

Alvirah had phoned Regan as soon as she hung up with Jack and told her about Alvin Luck. "Jack will call you the minute they find him," she promised. Then, on learning about Nora's short story, she had instantly volunteered to help in the search through the boxes in the attic.

Leaning on her crutches, with Willy on one side and Regan on the other, Nora made her careful way along the walk and into the house.

"When I left here Wednesday evening, I

never dreamed I'd come back this way. Or without Luke," she added, her tone flat.

The house seemed dark and somber. Regan quickly moved around, turning on lights. "Mom, where do you think you'd be most comfortable?" she asked.

"Oh, inside." She gestured toward the family room.

Alvirah took in every detail of the place as they followed Nora past the living room to the back of the house. The large kitchen spilled into the high-ceilinged family room, inviting with its generous couches, big windows, and open-hearth fireplace. "This is lovely," she said admiringly.

Nora hobbled over to the wing chair. Regan took her crutches, and when Nora was settled, helped lift the leg with its heavy cast onto the hassock. "Whew," Nora said with a sigh as she leaned back. "This is going to take some getting used to." The tiny beads of perspiration on her forehead were a testimony to the effort it had taken just to navigate the short distance from the car.

A few minutes later, after Willy and Regan had brought a half-dozen boxes down from the attic, they were all busy looking for the manuscript or magazine copy of the short story Nora remembered being titled "Deadline to Paradise."

"I thought I'd kept every piece of research, every version of every manuscript, every outline, even every rejection slip from the early days," Nora commented. "So where is it?"

As the four of them sifted through the stacks of papers, Alvirah told them about tracking down Alvin Luck. "I can't believe that anyone who's been working as a department store Santa Claus could be part of all this," Nora said. Then they all fell silent. Half an hour later, Willy and Regan went back up to the attic to bring down more boxes. But it was a fruitless effort. At three o'clock, Nora said dispiritedly, "I may as well admit it. If a copy of that story still exists, it isn't in this house." Then she looked at Regan. "Why don't you call Rosita's and see how her boys are doing? I'm worried about them."

From Fred's tone, Regan could tell immediately that it was not going well. "They're worried that their mother is sick," he told her. "All I'm trying to do at this point is keep them distracted. I even opened the package of books your mother sent them for Christmas and read to them. Those, at least, they really enjoyed."

"I'm glad they liked the books," Nora said after Regan reported what Fred had told her. "I had Charlotte in the children's section of the bookstore put them together and send them over for me." She paused. "Wait a minute. She also sent me videos of some of the hot new movies for kids. I was going to give them to Mona." Nora gestured toward the neighboring house. "Her grandchildren are coming for a visit next week."

She looked at Regan. "Why don't you take them to Chris and Bobby? Then if you get a chance to talk to Rosita at four o'clock, you can tell her you just saw the boys."

Regan looked at her watch. She was supposed to receive the next phone call at four. It wasn't much more than a fifteen-minute drive to Rosita's. That gave her over an hour to get there and back. She knew her mother wanted her to be home when the next call from the kidnappers came. She said that just knowing her husband was on the other end of the phone made the nightmare seem a little less hopeless.

Alvin Luck and his mother could not have spent a better day together. That is, until they got home and found two detectives waiting for them.

"May we speak to you inside?" they asked.

"Sure, fellows, come on in," Alvin invited. With the security that comes from having led an absolutely blameless life, he was thrilled that real-life detectives had come to talk to him. Maybe something had happened at Long's, and they needed his help.

His mother did not share his excitement. When the detectives asked permission to look around the apartment, she glared at Alvin for granting it.

Sal Bonaventure, the detective who went into Alvin's bedroom, whistled softly when he saw the accumulation of crime literature that was stacked floor to ceiling. Piles of manuscripts crowded the shelves over the long table that served as a desk.

In addition to a computer and printer, the table held dozens of books and magazines, most of them clearly very old. A stack of novels by Nora Regan Reilly, many of them lying open, was near the computer. Bonaventure saw that the pages were heavily annotated.

Sal and his partner had contacted Jack Reilly as soon as Alvin and his mother stepped into the entryway. He had told them to hold off on questioning until he got there.

Santa Claus may be the key to breaking this case wide open, Sal thought optimistically.

The snowstorm, predicted to hit earlier, finally had started—and with a vengeance—by the time Regan parked in front of Rosita's apartment. Fred Torres had been watching for her. "I told Chris and Bobby that you have some great new movies for them," he said heartily as he opened the door.

The boys were sitting on the floor, a dozen marbles scattered between them. They looked at Regan with some distrust.

"When is your mommy going to be better so our mommy can come home?" Chris asked.

He's trying to be polite, poor kid, Regan thought, but he wants an answer. "Very soon," she told him as she held out the gaily wrapped package of tapes. "This is for both of you . . ."

Her voice trailed off; she did not notice when they took the present from her hands. She was staring down at the cover of one of the books lying on the coffee table. The title *The Little Red Lighthouse and the Great Gray Bridge* had caught her eye and evoked a flood of memories.

Daddy, read this one again, just once more, please.

The cover illustration was of a jaunty red lighthouse. She opened the book. The frontispiece depicted the unmistakable George Washington Bridge, with the tiny lighthouse tucked below it.

Your favorite book . . . I'm seeing red . . .

This was what Dad was trying to tell me, Regan realized with mounting excitement. From wherever he is, he can see the lighthouse.

"Regan, what is it?" Fred asked urgently.

Regan shook her head. "I hope you guys enjoy the movies. I'll see you later." She turned to Fred.

"I'll walk you outside," he said.

The tension emanating from C.B. had accelerated to an explosive level. Luke and Rosita silently observed his grim countenance as the time for making the phone call drew near. He knows this is it, Luke thought. He knows that if they don't get the money tonight, they never will. He could hear the winds building up outside. The boat was banging against the pier with ever-increasing force. If this storm keeps up, who knows when and if their flight will take off.

"Hey, C.B.," Petey said, "I gotta run home. I left my passport in the apartment."

No you didn't, Luke thought. I saw you looking at it a little while ago. What was Petey up to now? he wondered.

"You what?" C.B. stared at him.

"I wanted to be sure it was in a nice safe

place. I don't have much room here. You've been sleeping home these couple of nights, I notice. What's the difference? It's a five-minute walk. Pick me up at the apartment."

C.B. looked at his watch. "Be waiting outside at precisely ten minutes after four."

"Gotcha." Petey looked from Luke to Rosita. "We may not ever meet again, but I'd like to wish you all the luck in the world." With a snappy salute, he was gone.

Luke knew why his feet were feeling cold and damp. There was a trickle of water on the floor. The ice, he thought. This tub is beginning to leak.

Jack Reilly's immediate gut feeling was that Alvin Luck was no threat to mankind. He was a mystery buff, not a kidnapper. Nora Regan Reilly was just one of many writers he collected.

Any question he or the detectives asked Alvin was answered promptly and without hesitation. He acknowledged that he had taken the picture of Luke at a mystery-writers' dinner. He had bought the frame after he heard about Nora's accident.

"Didn't she like it?" he asked as they stood in his cluttered bedroom.

"I know why they're asking you all these questions," his mother butted in. "You didn't sign your name to the card." She shook her head vigorously. "They don't like that kind of stuff. They think it means you have something to hide."

"Mrs. Reilly was just surprised to receive an unsigned gift," Jack said soothingly. "You did buy the teddy bear in the gift shop yourself?"

"What teddy bear?" his mother asked. "Alvin, you didn't say word one about any teddy bear."

"I see you've written a lot of notes in the margins of Mrs. Reilly's books." Jack picked up one of them and flipped through the pages.

"Oh, yes," Alvin said excitedly. "I've studied hundreds of mystery writers to see how they plot. It's a great learning tool. I file my notes under categories like murder, arson, burglary, embezzlement. When I read about true cases in the newspapers, I clip them out for my files too."

"Is that why you have these notes on Nora Regan Reilly?"

"Of course."

"Any chance you ever read 'Deadline to Paradise'?"

"That was one of her earliest stories. I filed it under kidnapping." He walked around the bed to a file cabinet and pulled open the bottom drawer. "Here it is." He handed Jack a thirty-one-year-old magazine.

Regan drove as swiftly as she dared over roads that were rapidly becoming snow covered. *Dad and Rosita can see the little red lighthouse,* she thought with a glimmer of hope. *They're somewhere around the George Washington Bridge.* Jack had said that background sounds on the tapes indicated that they were near water.

She dialed Jack's number.

"I just spoke to your mother and told her that Alvin Luck has been eliminated as a suspect. But he might turn out to be a big help—he had a copy of her story."

"What?"

"He's a serious mystery collector. If by

any wild chance the kidnappers follow the route used in the story, it'll be a lot easier to cover them."

"I have something to tell you too." Regan relayed to him what had just happened at Rosita's.

"Regan, this probably means they're being kept in New Jersey."

"Why?"

"Think about it," Jack said. "Your father left the hospital a little after ten. The car obviously was driven to New Jersey, because it came back across the George Washington Bridge into New York at 11:16. Then it crossed the Triborough Bridge into Queens at 11:45, which is just about how long it would normally take to travel that distance without stopping. If they didn't stop right after crossing the bridge into Manhattan, there's no way they could still see the lighthouse beyond that."

"For some reason, that makes me feel good," Regan said. The net is tightening, she thought.

Petey nursed a tequila sunrise at Elsie's Hideaway, where the annual Christmas

Eve party was in full swing. The whole gang of regulars was there. I'll just have *one* of these, he promised himself. I've got to have my wits about me for the big night.

If C.B. knew I'd stopped in here, he'd kill me. But I couldn't leave the U.S. of A. forever without one last visit to this joint, where, like the song says, "everybody knows your name." I've gone fishing with some of these guys, he thought. Lotta laughs.

"Petey, you look down in the dumps." Matt, Elsie's longtime bartender, replaced his empty tequila glass. "Elsie says 'Merry Christmas.' "

"Aw, that's nice."

"I hear you're going away on vacation. Where to?"

"Going fishing."

"Where?"

"Down south," Petey said vaguely.

Matt was already with the next customer.

Petey checked his watch. It was time to go. He slid off the bar stool, looked at the free tequila sunrise, and with uncharacteristic resolve, left it untouched.

"Petey, do you feel all right?" Matt looked concerned as he poured cocktail peanuts into an empty dish.

"I feel great," Petey assured him. "Like a million bucks."

"Glad to hear it. Have a good time on your trip. Send us a postcard."

"Say, do you have any more of those Elsie's postcards?" Petey asked.

Matt reached under the bar. "We've got one left. Be my guest."

With a wave, Petey left Elsie's for the last time.

Regan had kept Austin Grady up to date with everything that had been happening. For the last two days, he had been fielding calls from friends of the Reillys who had heard about Nora's accident and couldn't reach her or Luke.

When Nora phoned Austin at 3:15, he asked if he could stop by the house on his way home. Nora quickly responded, "I'd like to see you, Austin. You're the only one of our friends who knows what's going on."

Austin had been there only a few moments when Regan came in and told them about seeing the book about the red lighthouse.

"The Little Red Lighthouse and the Great Gray Bridge," Nora said. "Of course! You loved it."

"They've got to be in view of that lighthouse," Alvirah said emphatically. "There's no doubt that on those tapes he emphasized the words, 'I'm seeing red.' "

"Well, Jack thinks they're on the New Jersey side of the bridge," Regan said, and then explained why.

"If we only had some idea who did this," Nora said hopelessly. "But we have nothing else to go on, and they're calling in less than half an hour. Once they get the money, can we trust them to keep their end of the deal?" She gestured toward the window. "Look at the weather. If they did drop that bag by mistake yesterday, think of how much could go wrong today."

They all jumped when the doorbell rang.

"Regan, we can't have anyone else here. Say I'm sleeping . . ."

"I know, Mom." Regan hurried down the hall to the front door. Standing outside was the plant society president who had knocked on the window of Austin's office two nights ago. He was wearing a stocking cap, the top of which was slowly piling up with snow.

"Hi, Regan!" he chirped. "Remember me? I met you the other night. Ernest Bumbles."

He was carrying a gift-wrapped package under his arm.

"Hello, Mr. Bumbles," Regan said hurriedly.

"Is your dad here?" he asked.

"I'm afraid not," Regan said. "He was delayed in New York."

"Oh, what a shame. My wife and I are on our way to visit her mother in Boston. Although with this weather, no one should be out driving! Anyway, I have this gift I have so been wanting to give to your dad. It breaks my heart that I keep missing him. But I want him to have it for Christmas."

"Let me take it then," Regan said, anxious to end the conversation and get back to the others.

"Could you do me a favor?" Ernest asked with a pleading look.

"What's that?"

"Could you please open my gift to your

father now and let me take a picture of you with it?"

Regan felt like strangling him. She invited him to step inside, then quickly ripped off the ribbon and opened the box to find the framed proclamation.

"What's this for?" she asked as she read it.

Ernest beamed. "Your father has done so much for the Blossoms. He introduced Cuthbert Boniface Goodloe to our society. The poor man died just this week, but he left us a million dollars in his will. We can never thank your father enough."

"A million dollars?" Regan said.

Ernest looked misty eyed. "A million dollars. Virtually his entire estate! What a generous man. And it's *all* because of your father. We also have one of these citations to present to Mr. Goodloe's nephew, in honor of his wonderful uncle, but he's never home either! Now let me take your picture."

At Nora's request, Austin came down the hall from the family room to see what was going on. Oh my God, he said to himself when he spotted Bumbles. This guy never quits.

He caught Regan's eye but was stopped from brushing Bumbles off by the slight shake of her head.

Regan held up the citation. "Austin, look at this," she said with a forced bright smile. "My dad's the reason Mr. Bumbles' society received a million dollars this week from a Cuthbert Boniface Goodloe. Did you know my dad was directly responsible for that?"

Austin shook his head. "I had no idea."

"I was so sorry your dad had to miss our benefactor's funeral," Bumbles continued. "But the Blossoms showed up in full force."

"It's good you were there," Austin said. Regan has the patience of a saint, he thought. "His nephew is his only family."

"He is?" Regan said. She looked at Ernest and asked jokingly, "How did he feel about his uncle leaving such a big gift to the Blossoms?"

Ernest put his finger to his cheek. "I couldn't say. But why wouldn't he be happy for us? We're a wonderful society. And he'll be thrilled to receive one of these citations, I'm sure. That is, if I can ever reach him."

"Where does he live?" Regan asked.

"Fort Lee."

Regan swallowed hard. The New Jersey side of the George Washington Bridge was in Fort Lee. Was it possible? "I know my father will love this."

"Well, I'm just glad you're home to receive it. I'm keeping the other one in the trunk of my car so I can drop it by when I reach that nephew."

"Give it to me," Regan said. "I mean, I'm going to be in the vicinity of Fort Lee tonight, and I'll drop it at his house so he'll have it for Christmas too."

"That would be wonderful!" Ernest cried. "But I don't have his address."

"I'll call the office," Austin said. "I'm sure we have it on file."

"I'll be right back," Ernest said as he turned, went outside, and half slid down the path to his car, where Dolly was patiently waiting. When he returned, he handed Austin the other gift. "Hold this, please." He turned to Regan as he readied his camera. "Now say cheese."

"Cheese."

"Got it."

"What's the nephew's name anyway?"

Austin and Ernest answered in unison. "C.B. Dingle."

"I win," Bobby said halfheartedly. "Now let's put in the tape."

"First we've got to collect all these marbles," Fred told him.

The three of them crawled on their hands and knees and gathered the marbles that were scattered all over the living room. "I think I saw one go under the couch," Fred said. He lifted the skirt of the slipcover and ran his hand around in the narrow space between the couch and the rug. His groping fingers closed over the marble, but he could tell that it was resting on a smooth paper surface, not the carpeting. Sliding the paper out, he realized that it was a postcard addressed to Rosita.

The scrawled message was surrounded by dabs of colorful paint. It read:

Hope we can have dinner here
soon!!!!!!
                              Petey

Chris was standing beside Fred. He looked at the postcard. "Mommy was so funny when she got that card. She said that guy's elevator doesn't go to the top."

Fred smiled. "Did you ever meet him?"

Chris looked at Fred as though surprised he would ask such a dumb question. "Noooo! Mommy met him at work."

"He works for Mr. Reilly?"

"Just once. He painted something there. They hated the color."

Fred turned the card over. ELSIE'S HIDE-AWAY. EDGEWATER, NEW JERSEY. His heart skipped a beat. Flecks of paint in the abandoned limo. A guy who had worked for Luke Reilly and had been turned down by Rosita. A guy who obviously frequents a bar in the area of the George Washington Bridge.

"Start the tape," he told the boys. "I have to go in the bedroom to make a phone call."

Having bid farewell to Mr. Bumbles, Regan and Austin carried the gifts back to the family room.

"Well, this certainly supplies motive,"

Nora said as she read the proclamation. "But it could be another Alvin Luck situation."

"I wish we had more time," Regan said urgently. "I'd love to go up there and check him out. But the call is coming in ten minutes, and I probably will have to leave right away for New York. Jack is going to meet me with the second batch of money."

The ring of the phone went through the room with the impact of a gunshot.

"They wouldn't call on this line, would they?" Regan asked as she ran to the phone.

It was Fred.

She listened. "Hold on, Fred." She turned to Austin. "Fred just found a postcard from a guy named Petey, who apparently did some painting at the funeral home. He had asked Rosita out. Do you know who I'm talking about?"

Austin nodded. "We only had him work there one day. He completely messed up the job." Austin paused for a moment and then exclaimed, "But wait a minute! He showed up the other night at the wake for

Goodloe. He's a big buddy of C.B. Dingle."

Nora gasped. "He's a painter, and there
were flecks of paint in the limo."

"And the postcard he sent Rosita is of a
bar in Edgewater," Regan said. "That's
just south of Fort Lee and still within view
of the lighthouse."

Regan told Fred what they had learned
about C.B. Dingle.

"What's Petey's last name?" Fred almost barked into the phone.

"Austin, do you know Petey's last
name?"

He shook his head. "But hold on. I'll get
it for you." He picked up his cell phone
and called the office. "They're checking
the files." A moment later he said, "His
name is Peter Commet. He lives in Edgewater." Austin wrote down the address
and handed it to Regan.

"Fred, here it is," she said and gave him
the information. "They're calling me in two
minutes. I'll get back to you as soon as I
speak to them."

"Regan, I'm going looking for this guy,"
Fred said.

"I wish I could go with you."

At exactly four o'clock, her cell phone rang.

"Be at the Manhattan end of the Midtown Tunnel at 5:30."

"The Manhattan end of the Midtown Tunnel," she repeated, and looked at Nora.

"They're using my story," Nora breathed.

"I just brought my mother home from the hospital," Regan said rapidly. "I'm in New Jersey. I need more time than that."

"You can't have more time."

Austin put his hand on Regan's arm. "Let me go," he mouthed.

Regan nodded gratefully. "I'm not a good driver in this weather," she explained. "Is it okay if my father's associate, Austin Grady, delivers the money? He'll drive my car and use my phone. It won't do you any good if I have an accident."

There was a pause. Then she heard a reluctant, "All right. But for your father's and Rosita's sake, you better not be trying anything. Yell hello, you two."

For a brief instant she heard their voices in the background. *We're getting closer to you,* she wanted to shout. The phone clicked off.

She dialed Fred.

"I'm going up to Edgewater," Fred said. "And Alvirah and I are going to Fort Lee."

"Can I drop the kids with your mother?"

Regan hesitated. "Don't they think . . ."

"I'll tell them Rosita's doing an errand with your dad. By tomorrow they're going to have to be told the truth anyhow."

Regan gave him directions to the house. "Give me your cell-phone number. Take down my mother's. It's the one I'll have with me. Austin will be using mine."

"We'll keep in touch," Fred said. "Be careful."

"Weather's pretty bad out there," C.B. told Luke as he clicked off the phone. "Your daughter's too nervous to drive in it, so she's sending that guy Grady."

Regan can drive in any weather, Luke thought. Is Nora all right? Is something else up?

There was an air of finality in the way C.B. looked around the cabin. He took the keys to their chains from his pocket and laid them on top of the stove, well beyond their reach.

"When we get the money, you get to go home. Once we're safely away, we'll let them know where you are."

"Unless you want to kill us, you'd better do it soon," Luke said, indicating the floor of the boat. The storm outside had intensified, and the boat was rocking with ever-increasing force. The thumping, scraping sound of ice chunks hitting its sides was becoming more frequent. The floor was completely wet.

"We'll call from the airport. As soon as we land."

"That's too long," Rosita cried. "You might not get out until tomorrow."

"You'll just have to pray that we do," C.B. said. The door slammed behind him.

At ten minutes of five, Regan and Alvirah parked in front of C.B.'s high-rise apartment building. "Here we go," Regan said as they got out.

The doorman rang to announce them.

Moments later he shook his head. "No answer. He must be out."

"His uncle died this week," Regan said.

"I heard."

"My father owns the funeral parlor that handled the arrangements and has to get in touch with Mr. Dingle. It's very important. Is there any way I could find out when he's expected?"

"The superintendent's wife cleans his apartment. I could call her," the doorman offered. "That's the best I can do."

"Thank you," Regan said. "That's very nice of you." She and Alvirah exchanged glances.

"Hey, happy to help," he said with a shrug. "It's Christmas."

A minute later he turned back to them. "Dolores said to go up to her place. She's in 2B."

Dolores's apartment was a cheerful reminder of the holiday season. The tree was lit, Christmas music was playing, the smell of roast chicken was in the air.

"We won't keep you," Regan said hurriedly, "but we do need to be in touch with Mr. Dingle."

Dolores, a woman in her late fifties,

sounded sympathetic as she said, "Poor fellow. He told me he's taking a trip to make himself feel better. He was packing when I went up there this morning."

"You were up there this morning?" Alvirah asked.

"Not for long. I brought him some Christmas cookies. He invited me in for just a minute, but he seemed nervous and upset, like he was under a lot of stress. It'll do him good to get away."

"I'm sure it will," Regan said. Could they be hidden in a bedroom up there? she wondered.

"This building is lovely," Alvirah commented as she looked past her. "You have a wonderful view of the river. Is Mr. Dingle lucky enough to have one like this?"

"Oh no," Dolores said, smiling with a hint of superiority. "He has one of the small studios that face the street."

At quarter after five, snow swirling around him, Fred Torres was standing on the stoop of the shabby, two-family frame house in which Petey lived. Regan had called him after leaving C.B.'s building, saying that the only thing she had learned for sure was that he had left with his suitcases this morning, supposedly for a vacation. Luke and Rosita had almost certainly not been in his apartment.

Could they be here? Fred wondered as he rang the doorbell a second time. He had already tried the separate entrance to Petey's basement apartment, but it was dark inside, and no one answered.

Someone's upstairs, he thought. Lights were on, and he could hear the sound of a television.

The door was opened by a sleepy-looking man who appeared to be in his sixties. He was wearing rumpled jeans, an open flannel shirt, and bedroom slippers. He looked as though the bell had just awakened him. He did not seem pleased at the interruption.

"Are you the landlord of this building?" Fred asked.

"Yeah. Why?"

"I'm looking for Petey Commet."

"He left on vacation this morning."

"Do you know where he was going?"

"He didn't say, and it's none of my business." The landlord started to close the door.

Fred pulled out his police ID. "I need to talk to you about him."

The sleepy look vanished. "He in trouble?"

"I don't know yet," Fred replied. "How long has he been living here?"

"Three years."

"Ever had any problem with him?"

"Except for being late with the rent, not really. I know he'll come up with it eventually."

"Just a couple more questions and I'll let you go," Fred said. "Does he have any close friends around here?"

"If you count that gang at Elsie's Hideaway, he's got lots of them. It's right around the corner. Hey, I'm getting cold."

"One more thing. Have you been down in his apartment in the last couple of days?"

"Yeah, I checked the thermostat after he left this morning. If he isn't going to be here, no use burning fuel—not at today's prices."

This time Fred did not stop him from closing the door. As he got in his car, Regan and Alvirah were pulling up alongside him.

"No luck here either. But follow me to Elsie's Hideaway."

Because time was tight, Jack Reilly made the transfer of money to Regan's car a few blocks from the Queens-Midtown Tunnel. "We'll be following you," he told Austin Grady, "but if he directs you the way we expect, our mobile unit will have to drop back. It's just too easy for them to be seen. We've got agents deployed in the buildings along the route. They'll track you. Good luck."

At 5.30 the call came in. "Drive through the tunnel. Stay to the right. Take the Borden Avenue exit immediately after the toll booth."

"That's what we wanted to hear," Jack said exultantly when Eagle base passed on the message.

His cell phone rang. It was Regan. "Both the nephew and the painter left with their suitcases today. They told people they were going on vacation."

Jack felt a rush of adrenaline. "Regan,

I'll bet you anything that they're our guys.
If they have suitcases with them, that
means they're not going back to where
they left your father and Rosita. After they
pick up the money, they're probably
headed to the airport."

"If they get away, we may never hear
from them again."

"We'll keep them in sight, just in case
they do go back to where they have your
dad and Rosita, but the minute they hit either of the airports, we have no choice but
to close in on them."

"Alvirah and I are heading to the bar in
Edgewater where the painter hangs out.
Fred Torres is with us. Maybe somebody
there will be able to tell us something."

"Regan," Jack said quietly. "Please be
careful."

There was a crash followed by a startling
lurch as the boat listed to a twenty-degree
angle. Rosita and Luke were thrown to the
side. Rosita cried out, and Luke winced as
the manacles dug into his hands and an-
kles.

"Mr. Reilly, this boat is sinking! We're going to drown," Rosita sobbed.

"No we're not," Luke insisted. "I think one of the mooring lines gave way."

Less than a minute later, the boat was savagely hurled against the dock again.

Luke heard a gurgling sound, and water began to bubble from somewhere near the door. As the boat swayed once more, the ring of keys C.B. had left on the stove slid off and dropped to the floor. Desperately, Luke bent as far as the chains would allow and leaned forward. His finger touched the edge of one of the keys, but before he could attempt to grasp it, the boat pitched again, and the keys slid well beyond his reach.

Up until that moment, Luke had believed they had a chance, but not anymore. Even if C.B. made that call from wherever he was going, it would be too late. The water was rising steadily. Rosita was right—they were going to drown. Their bodies would be found chained like trapped animals, if they were found at all. This tub would be driftwood before much longer.

I had wanted a lot more years, he

thought, as the faces and voices of Nora and Regan permeated his soul.

From across the cabin, he could hear Rosita whisper, "Hail Mary, full of grace . . ."

He finished the prayer with her. ". . . at the hour of our death, Amen."

Inside Elsie's Hideaway, things were hopping. Regan, Fred, and Alvirah took only a moment to orient themselves, then headed straight to the bar.

Matt the bartender came over to them. "What can I get for you?"

"A couple of answers." Fred pulled out his police ID. "You know Petey Commet?"

"Sure I do. He was sitting right where you are less than two hours ago."

"According to his landlord, he left with his suitcases this morning," Fred said.

"Maybe he did, but he was here this afternoon. He did say he was going on vacation."

"Do you know where? It's important."

"I'd like to help you, but to tell you the truth, he was kind of vague about it. Said he was going fishing down south." Matt paused. "I don't know if this means any-thing, but Petey didn't seem like Petey to-day. I asked him about it, but he said he felt like a million bucks."

Regan's blood ran cold. "Can you tell us anyplace where he might have been hang-ing out between leaving his apartment this morning and coming in here a few hours ago?"

Matt shrugged. "He takes care of some-body's boat at the year-round marina in Weehawken. Maybe he decided to check it out before he takes off. He hangs out there sometimes."

"I know that place." Fred flipped open his cell phone. "Get me the number of Lincoln Harbor In Weehawken," he snapped.

A moment later he was speaking with the marina office. Regan could see the muscles in his face tighten. Whatever they're telling him, it isn't good news, she thought.

Fred finished the call and turned to Re-gan and Alvirah. "He took the houseboat out Wednesday afternoon and never came back. The woman I spoke to said he must be nuts. The ice is coming down the

river. No boats should be out in these conditions, especially an old tub like that."

Alvirah put a comforting hand on
Regan's arm as Fred put in a call to the
Harbor Unit.

Matt, who had been busy making
drinks, came back. "I've got an idea. Most
of these people know Petey, and a lot of
them work around here. Maybe they know
something."

He jumped up on the bar and whistled.
The crowd roared its approval. "Free
drinks for everyone," someone yelled.

Matt waved his hands at them. "You already got free food tonight. Now this is
important. Did anybody see Petey Commet around town today before he came in
here?"

Please, God, Regan thought. She
watched as people glanced at each other
and shook their heads. Then someone
called, "When I got off work, I drove
straight here. I saw Petey coming up that
path next to the Slocum Marina."

"That marina's closed for the winter.
Why would he go there?" a customer near
Regan mumbled.

Regan turned to him. "Where exactly is his marina?" she demanded.

"Go outside and make a left. It's a few blocks down on the right. You'll see the sign at the turn."

Fred, Regan, and Alvirah raced outside to Fred's car. He roared out of the parking lot, skidding on the snow-covered pavement.

"If they're on an old boat in this weather . . ." Regan didn't complete the thought.

"You just passed the turn!" Alvirah cried.

Fred did a U-turn and barreled down the steep, deserted road that led to the river. The wind-whipped snow reduced visibility to near zero. The road ended in a deserted parking lot. The headlights of the car penetrated the pall of snow enough for them to tell that the marina was empty. There was no boat in sight.

Fred grabbed a flashlight from the glove compartment and jumped out of the car. Followed by Regan and Alvirah, he hurried past the closed marina office. From somewhere off to the left they could hear a thumping, banging noise. Slipping and sliding in the wet snow, they rounded the corner and began to run. The powerful beam of the flashlight revealed a listing houseboat, slamming back and forth against the dock where it was moored. It looked as though it was about to sink.

"Oh my God," Regan screamed. "They're in there, I know it." She and Fred raced along the dock, Alvirah puffing behind them.

The line securing the boat to the dock was uncoiling from the cleat to which it was attached, and Fred grabbed and rewrapped it as best he could. "Alvirah, don't let this come loose."

"Dad!" Regan screamed as she made the dangerous jump onto the lopsided boat. "Rosita!" She began kicking the padlocked door.

At the sound of Regan's voice, Luke and Rosita thought they were dreaming. They were trying to keep their legs out of the icy water that was swirling along the floor. The bubbling leak had widened to a steady, gushing stream.

"Regan!" Luke shouted.

"Hurry!" Rosita screamed.

"We're coming," Fred shouted back. He was beside Regan.

Together they kicked the door repeatedly.

The wood panel finally splintered, then separated. They tugged and yanked at the loose wood until they managed to make an opening big enough to step through.

Fred went inside first, shining the flashlight into the pitch-black cabin. Regan followed him, wading into the deepening water, horrified at the sight of her father and Rosita chained to the walls.

"The keys were on the floor under the stove," Luke said urgently.

Fred and Regan bent over, frantically feeling around in the freezing water, which continued to rise steadily.

Please, please, Regan prayed. *Please!* Near the refrigerator, something metallic hit her hand but then was gone. "I felt them," she said. "Right around here."

Fred directed the beam of the flashlight at the base of the refrigerator.

"There they are!" Regan screamed as she lunged for them. Now the water was up to her knees. She snapped open the key ring and gave one key to Fred. She waded to Luke and grabbed his wrist. The key did not fit.

Fred turned away from Rosita, and they made the switch.

This time the keys worked.

Within seconds, both sets of chains were dangling. Supported by Regan, Luke stood up. Fred lifted Rosita to her feet.

"This boat won't last another thirty seconds," Fred said. "Let's get out of here."

The four of them sloshed through the water and stumbled through the shattered door.

Outside on the dock, a fervently praying Alvirah was hanging on to a rope that could no longer bear the strain of a sinking houseboat. As the boat slammed against the dock one final time, she braced herself. Summoning the strength she had used to move pianos in her cleaning-woman days, Alvirah held the rope taut until all four were safely beside her.

Then beaming, she watched as Regan and her father embraced, and Fred wrapped Rosita in his arms.

I knew he liked her, Alvirah thought happily.

Austin Grady followed the kidnappers' instructions to continue east on Borden Avenue and then make a left turn on to Twenty-fifth Street.

"Then pull over and wait," he was told. Austin drove slowly on the icy roads. The windshield wipers were barely able to keep up with the falling snow.

Twenty-fifth Street was dark and desolate, lined with old factory buildings that obviously had been closed for years. The phone rang again.

"Drive one block to Fifty-first Avenue and turn right. Go to the end of the street and pull over again. Leave the bag on the corner."

This is it, Austin thought. At the end of Fifty-first Avenue, he stopped the car, took out the bag with the million dollars, and placed it on the sidewalk. He got back in the car.

The cell phone rang again. "It's there," Austin said.

"Keep going. Make your left and get lost."

Jack was stationed four blocks away. His cell phone rang. It was Regan.

In a voice that was both tremulous and ecstatic, she said, *"We've got them! We're on our way home."*

Eagle base came on the radio. "Subjects picking up bag."

Jack keyed his transmitter. "Let's nail them."

Chris and Bobby were playing cards with Willy in the family room. Nora was sitting silently, staring into the fire. Numb with fear and anticipation, she jumped when the phone rang on the table next to her. She picked it up, terrified of what she might be about to hear.

"How's that leg of yours?" Luke asked.

Tears of relief coursed down her cheeks. "Oh, Luke," she whispered.

"We're all on our way." Luke's voice was husky with emotion. "See you in half an hour."

Nora hung up the phone. Chris and Bobby were looking at her expectantly. "Mommy's coming home," she managed to say.

C.B. and Petey, both of them handcuffed, were seated side by side in the back of the police car.

"It's not all my fault," Petey protested. "It was your uncle that died."

C.B. suddenly had the incongruous thought that maybe jail was preferable to a lifetime in Brazil with Petey.

Jack Reilly was dropped off at his apartment in Tribeca. He went directly to his car; his suitcases and presents were still locked safely in the trunk. Home for Christmas, he thought. All's well that ends well.

On the snowy, nearly deserted streets of Manhattan, he resumed the drive he had begun two nights before. He headed east, toward the FDR Drive. Then, as though of its own volition, the car made a U-turn.

Fred and Rosita followed Regan, Luke, and Alvirah as they pulled into the driveway. The cars had not yet stopped when the door of the house was flung open and two little boys came racing out, wearing neither coats nor shoes.

"Mommy! Mommy!" they screamed,

slipping and sliding as they ran down the walk.

Rosita threw off the blanket she'd been wrapped in, stumbled from the car, and scooped up in her arms the children she thought she would never see again.

"I *knew* you'd be home in time for Christmas," Chris whispered.

Bobby looked at her, his expression suddenly stricken. "Mommy, is it all right? We already decorated the Christmas tree. But we saved some of the ornaments for you to put on."

"We'll hang them on the tree together," Rosita assured him happily, as she hugged them to her.

Fred had stood back, but now he came over. "Which one of you guys do I get to carry inside?"

Luke and Regan and Alvirah opened their car doors. "Why isn't your mother running out to greet me?" Luke asked.

"Something about a rug I sent her."

They walked up the path together.

Willy was standing at the front door, waiting for Alvirah.

When Luke stepped inside his home, it was as though he were seeing it for the first time. "Home sweet home," he said fervently, then hurried back to the family room where Nora was waiting, Alvirah close at his heels. Willy grabbed her arm. "Give them a minute alone, honey."

"You're right, Willy. It's just that I'm a hopeless romantic."

Forty minutes later, warmed by hot showers and changed into dry clothes, the captives and their rescuers were back in the family room.

The spread Nora ordered from the local gourmet deli had just arrived. Regan, Alvirah, and Willy began setting up a buffet. Austin had called, proud to have played a part in saving his friend's life.

"I'll drop by with the family tomorrow," he said.

Nora, a glass of wine in her hand, announced, "We're going to throw a big celebratory party next week—and I'm inviting Alvin Luck."

"Isn't he the guy who sent you a present when my back was turned?" Luke asked.

Rosita was sitting on the couch with

Fred, the boys at her feet. She turned to him. "Will you be back in time?"

He looked at her and smiled. "Do you really think that after tonight I want to get on another boat?"

Rosita's smile was brilliant as he said, "I'm not going anywhere, Cinderella."

The doorbell rang.

"I bet it's that Ernest Bumbles," Alvirah said jovially.

"I'm having a citation made especially for him!" Nora declared. "Put his name on the party list, Luke."

Regan walked slowly to answer the door, the sounds of laughter spilling from the room behind her. She felt over-whelmed with gratitude, peace, exhaustion . . . And something else in her heart.

She opened the door. The man she had met only two nights ago in her mother's hospital room was smiling down at her.

"Have you got room for another Reilly around here?" asked Jack.